STRANGE WEATHER IN CHINATOWN

A Nick Thomas Adventure

PATRICK LIVANOS LESTER

Rhumbline

Strange Weather in Chinatown/ Patrick Lester—1st ed.

Book cover art and design by Patrick Lester

Print ISBN: 978-1-948992-06-0

Electronic ISBN: 978-1-948992-07-7

1.0

Rhumbline Press

Rhumb line. *noun.*

A path taken by a water craft or aircraft that maintains a constant compass direction.

For Genie Lester

Thanks to my editors and beta readers Genie Lester, Sandy Boucher, Ruth McDonnell, Brad Sheldon, and Debra Alderson.

My biggest thanks goes to Kim, for her constant support.

Truth is stranger than Fiction,
but it is because Fiction is obliged to stick to possibilities;
Truth isn't.

Mark Twain
Following the Equator

Chapter One

Nick Thomas always trusted people too easily. It came from his belief that people are basically good, and doing the right thing was, well, the right way to live. It was a trait instilled in him by his parents.

It had not always served him well.

I'll have to work on that, he thought as he gave the winch in front of him a small turn.

He looked up in time to spot a man on the sailboat ahead tumble over the side.

"Man overboard!" Nick shouted.

"Where is he?" yelled the captain.

"He's at one o'clock, ten yards," Nick called back to the helm. They were on *Bad Latitude*, a sailboat in the Honolulu Friday night yacht race. The boat headed downwind toward the H1 buoy marking the entrance to the Honolulu Harbor and their turning point in the race. Nick was in the cockpit, adjusting the sails. The boats flew spinnakers, brightly colored parachute-like sails used for running downwind.

Racers on other sailboats echoed "Man overboard." Boats

scattered, making room for the closest boats to avoid the man in the water.

"He's ten yards out. If you head up and ease the main, we can pick him up on the port side," Nick called, keeping an eye on the man in the water.

The captain eased the line controlling the mainsail as they sped toward the man.

"Five yards," Nick called.

Nick reached over the side, grabbed the out-stretched hand and hauled him in, catching the man's t-shirt on a cleat and tearing it off on his way to the cockpit floor, landing him with a thud.

A moment later, the captain yelled, "Prepare to drop the chute! We can still be first around the mark!"

There was a flurry of activity as the foredeck crew got ready to drop the spinnaker. The forward hatch popped open and a hand reached up, ready to haul the sail below deck.

"Drop the chute!" yelled the captain. "Jibing! Trim, trim!"

The boat turned. They hoisted the jib and dropped the spinnaker as they rounded the mark. The other boats were far behind them, trying to get back in the race and around the buoy without colliding with each other. Nick checked the jib and gave the winch a quarter turn. He glanced at the wet man lying on the floor of the cockpit, his head down, and curled in a ball, keeping out of the way.

The man looked up and said, "Hey, Nick. I thought I would see you today. Thanks for the rescue."

"Willie. I was planning to call you this week. And here you are."

"You know this guy?" asked the captain.

"Sure. He's one of my better friends."

"You guys act like this is a common occurrence, rescuing a friend in the middle of a race."

Nick and Willie looked at each other and shrugged. "Small island," they said in unison.

Nick turned to Willie. "Are we still sailing this Sunday?" Nick asked.

"We're sailing now," Willie said.

"What are you doing here? I thought you didn't like to race." Nick glanced up at the sail.

"Yeah, there's a reason for that. This is the first time I've been out on a race in years. It was a last-minute thing. I caught up with a friend in town and he invited me. I leaned back against the lifeline and it snapped. It was an awkward place for it to happen, right as we crowded in approaching the mark." Willie shook his head and sprayed the cockpit and Nick with water. "This is a stupid sport."

Later that night at the Waikiki Yacht Club, they were joined by Nigel, an Englishman, and the one who pulled the spinnaker through the hatch on the foredeck. Willie, the center of attention, had a line of drinks in front of him bought for him by other sailors. He was the celebrity of the moment and enjoying himself.

Willie looked around the club. "So this is where all the *haoles* are."

Nick and Nigel let out a laugh. The club was packed with sailors.

"I can't believe you do the *pau hana* race every Friday night," Willie said.

"Some Fridays are more exciting than others," Nick said.

"The driver of your boat—does he always yell orders like that?" Willie asked, sliding one of the drinks in front of him to Nick and another to Nigel.

Nick took a whiff and then a sip. *"Cuba Libre.* I haven't had one of these in years."

Nigel slid the drink back to Willie. "I'll stick to whisky, thanks."

"Yes, the captain always yells. It took some getting used to. He's highly competitive. We call him 'Bligh,'" Nick said.

Willie took a healthy swallow. "I noticed he didn't let a thing like rescuing a man slow him down."

"We did win the race," Nigel said, taking a sip of whisky.

"It's amazing what we will do for a cheap bottle of champagne," Nick said.

"And bragging rights, don't forget bragging rights," Nigel added.

Chapter Two

The following Sunday, a muggy August morning, Nick sat in the shade under the dodger on the stern of *Icarus*, his sailboat and home. He was drinking from a flask of water, cooling off after an early morning run down Waikiki beach, past the hotels and the zoo, through Kapiolani Park, and back to his boat docked in the Ala Wai Harbor.

Built in 1931, *Icarus* was a fifty-seven foot wooden yawl, designed by naval architect John G. Alden. Nick's grandfather had won the boat in a spirited game of poker in Nick's hometown of San Francisco shortly after World War II and christened her *Icarus*. The Greek myth of *Icarus* is one of the hubris of man. Nick's grandfather thought it the perfect name for a boat won in a game of chance.

He was that kind of man.

Icarus was all Nick had left of his San Francisco old-money family fortune. A year and a half earlier, he had leveraged his personal assets to expand his company. It seemed like a sure thing at the time; he thought nothing could go wrong. Then at the final hour of the transaction, Lance Grabowski, Nick's friend and business partner, emptied the company's bank accounts and disappeared along with thirty-two million dollars. Nick lost his homes, his cars, his plane, and even *Icarus*. And Jody—his wife— Lance took Nick's wife with him.

Adding to the pain of losing everything, the FBI investigated Nick in excruciating detail. That they considered him a suspect in his own embezzlement made no sense to him—or to John Mitchell, the agent investigating him. Lance and Jody had not been heard from or found, and neither had the money they had taken with them.

What Nick had left were family heirlooms he and his friend Jim packed into inexpensive self-storage in a remote cattle town in far-northern California.

Then Nick did what most men would *not* do. He took the rest of his cash—twelve hundred and seventy-five dollars and thirty-seven cents—and bought a plane ticket to Tahiti.

The first night in Papeete, Nick played piano with a jazz combo. The band members befriended him and gave him shelter and food. He even became a judge of the Miss Tahiti Contest. It was a good life—except for the immigration officer, who informed Nick it was time to leave French Polynesia.

Before Nick left Tahiti, he met James Dewey, a fellow judge at the contest. Dewey offered him a job in Honolulu preparing the start-up of an Australian airline beginning service to Hawaii.

Why did Nick still have *Icarus*? Katherine, his college girl-friend, and Lance's ex-wife, contacted Willie. Together, they bought *Icarus* from the creditors and had it sailed to Hawaii. Katherine came from an affluent family, but unlike Nick, she had kept her inheritance away from her spouse.

The job with the airline compensated Nick well, and when it ended, he worked as a freelance business consultant. Against her protests, Nick paid back Katherine for *Icarus* and set aside a small pile of cash. He began paying Willie back with a low interest loan. Willie still owned a portion of *Icarus* as he had put his name in for a slip in the Ala Wai boat harbor many years ago. A live-aboard slip became available and the timing had been perfect.

Nick glanced up at the dodger he had made from a shredded sail a boat owner threw away after a particularly raucous race. The high-tech, high-performance Kevlar sail made a beautiful ceiling that covered the entire cockpit and a good part of the boat. Nick had trimmed it to fit and hand-stitched a hem to keep it from fraying. It dropped the temperature below the deck and extended his outdoor living in all types of weather.

As he sipped water, Nick surveyed the bizarre collection of boats on the live-aboard dock. There was a Chinese junk, a converted tugboat, and two houseboats, one with Adirondack chairs on the roof positioned under a red umbrella. Sailors added over-water decks at their slips with tables and chairs, awnings, and barbecues. One slip had an outdoor kitchen with a tile floor. The harbor was filled with the names of boats one sees in every harbor: *Serenity, Island Time, Nauti and Nice, Day O, The Other Woman, Aquaholic*, and of course a host of Hawaiian versions: *Pau Hana* (After Work), *Kuuipo* (Sweetheart), and *Nalu* (Wave).

Nigel lived nearby on a boat named *Awkward Lizard*.

As true of most yacht harbors, the Ala Wai had its own community, and people looked out for one another. Nick was happy to be part of it.

It had been awhile since Nick lost nearly everything. He referred to it as his *Flat Broke* era. Lance destroyed his business, stole his money, and disappeared with his wife.

But Lance didn't get his boat.

Nick loved his boat.

Nick spent a half an hour unfastening the dodger and stowing it in the lazarette. He waited for Willie and the rest of the crew to show up for a late morning sail. *Icarus* had been in her slip for nearly a month and Nick was antsy to get her into blue water, raise the sails—blow the cobwebs out of the rigging. In a cold climate like San Francisco, where *Icarus* spent most of her life, he used a block heater to warm up the oil before attempting to start the diesel engine. In Hawaii, in the summer, it was unnecessary. He opened the hatch, checked the oil, and opened the intake valve. Back on deck, he made sure the transmission was in neutral, turned the key to ON, and pushed the starter button. The engine turned and caught. Over the side, water from the cooling system ejected overboard. He was taking the cover off the mainsail when he heard the noise. It started as a rattle and he rushed to turn off the engine. As he arrived at the console, he smelled oily smoke, and the rattle had turned into a series of loud clunks.

Then there was a *BANG* followed by silence.

"That didn't sound good," Willie said, standing at the dock. "In fact, that sounded really expensive."

"Hey, Willie. Come aboard," Nick said.

Willie and Nick headed to the cabin, and Nick turned on a fan to evacuate the smoke. Nick opened the panel to the engine compartment and took a flashlight from its cradle. They both got down on their knees and peered at the engine.

"Uh, oh," Willie said.

Nick ran a finger down the side of the engine block, feeling the jagged break. "I've never seen that happen before."

"As I said, that sounded expensive. I didn't think it would be *that* expensive. The block's cracked. How does that even happen?"

"The engine is a Detroit Diesel from the late 1950s. I figured it would last forever," Nick said.

"It's a write-off now," Willie said, shaking his head.

Nick sat down on the cabin floor and looked up at the companionway hatch. "I'll have to slide the engine from its compartment and hoist it out."

"I'll let the crew know we're not going out today," Willie said, pulling his phone from his seabag.

Chapter Three

The next day, Nick sat at the chart table working on his laptop, going over his accounts. Besides needing a new engine, *Icarus* was due for a haul-out, bottom scrape, and repaint. One doesn't want to mess with the maintenance on a wooden boat. Nick got online and did his research, entering the numbers into a spreadsheet. He felt a pit in his stomach. The repairs would drain his reserves, leaving *Icarus* stuck in her berth, a *dock queen,* until he replaced the engine.

It was clear to Nick he needed to get back to work and make some money.

He spent the next couple of hours sending emails to potential clients, inquiring if anyone needed a business consultant.

After lunch, Nick bicycled to San Souci Beach for a swim. Far enough away from the crowded beaches near the hotels of Waikiki, Sans Souci is often populated by residents. This day was no exception, and Nick nodded hello to a few faces he recognized. One fellow named Matt retired at twenty-eight after an industrial accident injured his back. He worked the stock market early in the morning and read investment information on the beach in the afternoon. There were lots of people like that at Sans Souci and one was likely to hear animated discussions of day-trading, commodity dealing, or currency trading.

Nick didn't know it, but he had a distant connection to Sans Souci Beach. George Lycurgus, a Greek citizen, made his way to Hawaii in the late 1800s where he leased a guest house on the beach not far from where Nick was sitting. Lycurgus increased the size of the place and renamed it *Sans Souci*. It has been called Sans Souci Beach ever since and became one of the first beach resorts in Waikiki, attracting such guests as author Robert Louis Stevenson.

In 1914, George Lycurgus returned to Greece to visit his family. The outbreak of World War I delayed his return to Hawaii until 1920. Nick's grandfather would meet Lycurgus on a ship sailing from Greece to New York, where they whiled away the hours onboard the *Megali Hellas* playing poker and smoking cigars. Nick had heard his grandfather talk of his friend George in Hawaii, but he never made the connection.

Uncle George, as Lycurgus was later known in Hawaii, befriended Hawaiian royalty and bought the Volcano House, an inn on the edge of the Kīlauea Caldera, on the island of Hawaii. There, he rubbed elbows with the top brass of the military during World War II. Like Nick's grandfather, Uncle George lived a long, full life. He passed on at his beloved Volcano House at the age of 101 or 102. History is murky on that point.

It was a clear day, and the windsock on the reef was limp. There were a few cirrus clouds on the horizon. Box jellyfish make their arrival five to seven days after the full moon. The moon was a waxing crescent, and Nick felt safe to swim his customary four laps to the windsock and back.

Showered and back in the shade, Nick picked up the *Penguin History of the World* by J. M. Roberts. He read for a while, then stopped to ponder what possessed ol' J. M. to take on documenting the whole of history.

Nick became aware of a group of people setting up camp directly behind his chair on the beach. He kept to his book until he could no longer concentrate, having read the same paragraph three times with none of it sinking in. The conversation behind him was distracting. The group was composed of ecdysiasts— they shed their clothing for money. Strippers. They were discussing in great detail their monetary earnings, club owners and corrupt police, the best single tip ($1000), breast enlargement and plastic surgery of all types imaginable, tattoos, and the pain of piercing certain portions of the anatomy. Nick gave up on reading and concentrated on eavesdropping. He scribbled notes in the book's margin as he listened and pretended to read. *Willie is going to love this,* Nick thought. He wondered what J. M. Roberts would think of the additions to his opus.

The crowd continued with a detailed and sophisticated investment discussion with an emphasis on long-term planning aimed at early retirement. That was followed by a discussion on the best countries to live when they retired.

"How can you do that for a living?"

Someone else was also eavesdropping. Nick glanced at the speaker to his left. She had a backpack open and books spread out on her beach towel. He assumed she was a college student.

"Don't you feel abused and exploited?" the student asked.

A silence fell. Finally, one woman spoke. "I'm sure there are some in our business that do. It depends on the club and the owner. Where I work, I'm in total control."

"But can't you find another way to make a living?"

"I have regular customers who are respectful, I make fantastic money, and I like what I do. I get paid a lot to keep in shape, and I'll be able to retire and do whatever I like in five years."

The student scoffed, "You could go back to school, get a college degree like me."

"I have an MBA from Columbia."

"That's weird. I still think it's creepy what you do."

The woman looked at her with a patient expression. "I'm sure you'll be successful with your college degree."

She turned back to her companions.

Forty-five minutes later, having fortified his gray matter and his curiosity a great deal, Nick set off to the gym. He glanced at the crowd as he packed up his gear. The tanned and toned women wore thong bikinis. One blonde with perfect teeth and in a neon pink bikini shot him a smile certain to collect big tips.

Chapter Four

A couple of days later, Nick's phone rang.

"Are you still on the beach?" Willie asked. It was just after 10:00 a.m., Willie's customary wake up time.

"Yes, I am currently without gainful employment." Nick was on *Icarus*, had already returned from a run, had breakfast, and was reading his email. He could hear Willie's espresso machine running in the background. It was a commercial unit he had installed at home, and for years the pump had been making a loud unpleasant whirring noise. Willie came to enjoy the noise and resisted the requests of his female overnight guests to repair it.

"There's a guy in town looking for someone to write a business plan for him. I thought of you."

"Thanks, Willie. I appreciate it. Does he shoot straight or is he one of those entrepreneurial maniacs?"

"If I recall, you are one of those entrepreneurial maniacs."

"True, but I like to think I am a straight shooter."

"You are a flippin' Boy Scout. I haven't met him; he lives next to a couple of my friends near the beach here on the Windward side."

"Please text me his number, and I'll give him a call," Nick said.

"Will do. I've got to go. Tell me Sunday how it worked out."

William Kekoa Wo Lee, known to his friends as *Willie*, grew up in the Kalihi District of Honolulu on the island of Oahu. His grandfather was Chinese-Hawaiian, and his grandmother Puerto Rican-Sicilian. Willie embraced each of these ethnicities and spoke the four languages of his ancestors, and Japanese, and of course, English. After Willie graduated from the elite Punahou School in Honolulu, he headed to the mainland for college. In San Francisco, he took up residence with an aunt and uncle in the Chinatown District and started school across the Bay at the University of California at Berkeley. There, in a Monday morning English class, he met Nick Thomas during their first semester. Nick and Willie connected immediately and became fast friends. Willie was a fixture at the Thomas family home in the Marina District of San Francisco. In turn, Willie gave Nick an entrée into Chinatown rarely shown to an outsider.

After graduating from Berkeley, Willie joined the family business of real estate investing. In real estate investing, timing is critical, and Willie's timing had been excellent. To say he made a killing was an understatement. In less than five years after graduating from Berkeley, Willie moved back to Oahu and bought a waterfront home on the Windward side of the island. He didn't need to work. He whiled away the tropical hours sailing on his boat, fishing, reading, going to the gym, and exploring a string of monogamous relationships.

Chapter Five

For his meeting with the entrepreneur, Nick dressed in the uniform of Hawaii business attire—trousers and a pressed aloha shirt, the shirt printed in a subtle pattern of ukuleles and sailboats.

He drove downtown and into Chinatown near the Honolulu waterfront. Some of the sidewalks were made from ballast stone of sailing ships that had moored in the harbor in the 1800s. With the only royal palace on American soil situated nearby, the territory has a distinctive flavor. Chinatown sits right on the fringe. It's compact, intense, and dangerous due to the rampant drug dealing and prostitution. The city occasionally cleans it up, but the neighborhood cycles from bad to better to bad at a surprising rate. It is not a place to walk alone after dark. Nick found a parking spot for his vintage Triumph near the front door of *Little Village Noodle House* and made his way into the building. He stepped inside and surveyed the scene, taking in the scent of spices and ginger. It was crowded and noisy. A man at a table near the window waved him over and motioned him to a chair.

Dressed in jeans, a black short-sleeve shirt, and cheap black flip-flops, or *slippers*, as they are called in the islands, Blaine Daniels was a large, round man of average height who had a soft feminine face with moist eyes and long eyelashes. He wore a turquoise and silver ring with a matching cuff. There were four platters of food on the table, still steaming. He had a plate piled high with food in front of him.

Nick looked at his watch. "I'm sorry, I thought you said noon for lunch."

"You're right on time. I went ahead and ordered," Blaine said. "You've got to try the taro duck. It's fabulous. I order it with extra sauce."

"All right." Nick sat down.

He served himself from the platters as Blaine continued eating, his silver and turquoise cuff clanking on the tabletop as he did. While they ate, they talked about living in Hawaii and the local business climate. Blaine told Nick he had been married four times and had lived in "lots of different places" without going into any detail. He then launched into an introduction to his business.

"I've been working in and around the entertainment industry for most of my life. I have a lot of contacts I can leverage."

Nick took a tentative bite of taro duck.

"So what's the business you have planned—to leverage your contacts?" Nick asked.

"Digital animation for motion picture and commercials. I'd also like to get into the medical billing business. I've come up with a cool way to automate it—to make it more efficient. There's a lot of money in anything medical."

Blaine took a big bite of an egg roll, breaking it apart. Much of it slid down his shirt, resting on his gut.

"I like the idea of multiple income streams," Nick said. "Although those are fairly disparate."

"Not really. It's software running on computers. The development teams have different skill sets, that's all."

Blaine had a conspiratorial way of speaking, as if he were letting you in on a secret. Nick could understand how people could find it charismatic. He wondered if it was an affectation.

Nick peppered Blaine with questions about his business model, the industry, the target markets, his short- and long-term goals for the business, how he would approach production, sales, marketing, and the exit strategy—those and other items that go into planning a business.

It was clear to Nick that Blaine had given little thought to the process, but he had reasonable answers.

Blaine didn't ask Nick about his background or abilities. He didn't appear interested. Nick figured Blaine had done due-diligence on him before the meeting. Nick had kept a low profile in Honolulu, working for the airline and traveling often. A quick search on the internet would reveal his trouble in San Francisco. After months of questioning, the FBI concluded he was no longer a suspect in embezzling his own money, or at least found no evidence to charge him with a crime. The case had been reported in the news and on-line for all the world to see—forever. He thought that might raise at least a few questions from someone wanting to hire him.

Before their meeting, Nick had gone online and researched Blaine Daniels. He found Daniels had won a minor award for software design, and nothing else.

"It's a bit premature, meeting you like this. The company hasn't secured funding, only seed capital," Blaine said, "But I have enough to give you an advance to write the business plan. What do you think?" Blaine asked.

Nick and Blaine agreed on a schedule and an hourly rate. Nick would write the business plan and provide a financial pro forma. Blaine offered a combination of cash and stock options. Nick declined the stock and renegotiated for cash. He had friends who had folders of useless stock from the dot-com era. They joked about wallpapering their bathrooms with the stock certificates. Besides, he needed the money for *Icarus*.

Blaine promised to email him the company information the following week. Until then, Nick would outline the plan and send Blaine a list of items he needed to complete it.

When Nick left the lunch meeting, he had a check for a sizable advance in his pocket. Life to him had never been about a paycheck, but satisfaction in his work. Nick didn't fool himself. He knew his attitude was from having been born into money.

Now, with *Icarus* in need of a haul out and serious repair, it was all about the money.

Chapter Six

With the advance for the business plan in hand and money in the bank, Nick focused on the repairs on *Icarus*. He had heard of a shipwright in Hawaii specializing in wooden boats, a Fijian considered by many to be the best in the Pacific. He called and made an appointment to get an estimate on the work.

The next day, Sam, the owner of the yard, requested permission to come aboard. He was a solidly built Fijian man with a calm voice and bright eyes. Nick took an instant liking to him.

Sam took his time inspecting *Icarus*. "Beautiful boat. She an Alden?" he asked, standing behind the wheel. Nick nodded. He kept the boat polished and in working order. Sam ran his fingers across the brightwork on the way down the companionway. Nick followed him.

Sam took a sniff. Nick knew he would smell no mold or rot. Sam saw everything in its place, stowed away, and the bunk made. He gave a slight smile.

"How long you have her?"

"Forever. She was my grandfather's boat, and then my father's. Now she's mine."

Another smile from Sam.

"She was re-caulked ten years ago, but she needs a coat of paint and other improvements. We already talked about the engine," Nick added.

Below, Sam peered into the engine compartment, saw the engine and winced.

"Never seen a block crack like that," Sam said.

"The engine's been well taken care of," Nick said, "Babied, really."

Sam sensed Nick's embarrassment.

"How old is it?"

"My grandfather put it in in the 1950s," Nick said.

"It's had a good long life. You shouldn't feel guilty about it." He stood back. "Do you want the same engine back in? I'd need to order it from the mainland."

"I'm open to suggestions," Nick said.

"If she were my boat, I'd upgrade it," Sam said.

After some discussion, they settled on a modern Volvo-Penta diesel that was lighter, more powerful, quieter, and smaller than the old Detroit Diesel. They reviewed the rest of Nick's repair list.

"What's next?" Nick asked.

"Let's get her out of the water and see how she looks on cradles."

Sam told Nick there was an opening at the boatyard the following week, but he needed to be ready to have the boat pulled out at a moment's notice to do the work between other jobs. They would haul out the boat and let Nick do repairs and maintenance while Sam's crew installed the engine. Nick needed to finish the job quickly to avoid expensive yard fees while *Icarus* was ashore. It was a good deal for Nick, who was trying to stay within his budget.

Chapter Seven

Nick needed a place to stay while the boat was up on blocks. Willie offered him a room, but it was in Kailua on the other side of the island. Traffic in Honolulu had become as unbearable as in any big city, and he wanted to be close to *Icarus* to check on the progress and do his own work on the boat. He considered getting a cheap hotel room in Waikiki, but after looking online figured it less expensive to rent a room for a month. He wanted slack built-in to his schedule in case there were surprises when he opened up *Icarus* while she was out of the water.

He took a trip to the university to check the bulletin boards for rooms to rent. As he drove by the University of Hawaii, he found the campus to be architecturally schizophrenic, with old plantation style buildings and big concrete block monstrosities built in the 1970s. It was an odd combination.

Nick was lucky to find parking on a side street. He got out and walked to the University where a group assembled on the corner, waiting to cross the street. In front of him was a girl who often sailed with him on Willie's boat on the weekends.

"Hi Charlotte," Nick said.

The girl turned to him. "Nick, what are you doing on campus?"

"Checking the bulletin boards for a place to stay while *Icarus* is hauled out."

"I'd let you stay with me and Tina if we had the space and our landlord was less strict."

"I appreciate that. I'm sure I'll find something."

Nick heard a bus come from behind and leapt back, pulling Charlotte with him. He fell on his back with her on top of him. She let out a screech as she fell; the bus jumping the curb where they had been standing. Other students yelled and screamed as they ran. The bus scraped the street light post and continued down the road, leaving a pile of bodies, untouched but shaken.

The students got up, pulling others with them.

"Thanks," Charlotte said, pulling Nick up with her.

"No problem."

The crowd was silent as they waited for the crosswalk light. The light changed and they crossed together, scattering once across the street and into the university.

"See you Sunday?" Charlotte asked.

"I'll be there," Nick said.

Nick made his way into the middle of the campus and scoured the bulletin boards in the student union. He saw an available room in a home in the back of Manoa Valley. He called the number and a woman told him there was lots of interest and he should come right away for a look. Nick headed back to his car and drove to the address she gave him.

The potential roommates were sisters, their mother a professor of classic literature at an East Coast liberal arts college. The elder, Cassandra, was home for lunch. She was welcoming, but firm, requesting references and financials before she would consider renting to him. Cassandra informed him if she approved, she needed to know his decision that day. Nick thought about it for a minute and decided to take the room, not wanting to miss the opportunity.

Nick had come prepared and retrieved a copy of his tax return from the car. It had been a good year working for the airline and later as a business consultant. Cassandra's eyes got big when she saw his gross income.

"I'm sure that will be fine," she said.

"I'll leave you the names and numbers of a few references."

The room contained a single bed, dresser, bedside table, lamp, desk, and chair. Cassandra had the master en suite and Nick would share the bath with the other sister, Persephone, who also went by *Persie*.

Nick sat on the bed. It was firm and looked new.

"Our previous tenant bought a new bed, and then just left when his rent came due. He probably spent all of his money on the mattress. I can get rid of the furniture if we come to an arrangement," Casandra offered.

"That's not necessary. This should be fine." It relieved Nick to find a furnished room. It saved him having to dig up furniture, or worse, sleep on an inflatable bed, or on the floor.

"You understand it's available immediately and only for a month. I lined up a friend for the long term. We need someone to help us cover expenses until then."

"I'm doing work on my place. It should be completed by

then." When Nick told people he lived on a boat, it led to lots of questions about life on board. He liked to keep his home life private.

That evening, after Casandra had contacted Nick's references, she called to tell him the room was his if he wanted it. He made plans to pick up the key and move in the next day.

Nick found it unnerving having an accurate time sense. He stirred and turned to the clock; it was a fuzzy 6:23 through the mosquito net, as it was each morning. It had been a cool night near the back of Manoa Valley.

Nick's custom was to wake up slowly, thinking of the day ahead. The previous week he had finished a consulting job, writing a grant proposal to the federal government for an underwater navigation system. He was once again a man of leisure, at least until Sam pulled *Icarus* from the water, and Blaine sent him the information he needed to get started on the business plan. The day would be filled with reading and drawing in his sketchbook until eleven, a bicycle ride to the local outdoor café, a leisurely ride back home, and then a drive to the beach around two, a swim and then a couple more hours of reading. At 4:00 p.m., the public gym opened at the community center and he would exercise for an hour. The evening called for a tennis game with Nigel and then dinner.

Nick heard a quiet scratching to his right. He turned, opened his eyes, and focused on a green gecko astride the clock on the outside of the mosquito net.

"Good morning, Zeke," he said to the critter. The lizard had been there for the last three mornings.

He rolled off the bed, padded to the kitchen, ground coffee

beans, and loaded and turned on the espresso machine. His roommates had left for work.

As he climbed into the free-standing bathtub and under the shower, he came eye-to-eye with another lizard perched on the shower head. Nick using his grandfather's brass shaving brush to lather and a razor to prune a day's growth. He dried off, retrieved his espresso and walked to the window looking out across the mossy deck. It promised to be a beautiful day in the islands. Manoa Valley was clear, even to the back of the usually cloudy rainforest. A cacophony of tropical squawking began deep in the valley and echoed forward. To Nick, it was as close to living in the jungle as was possible in civilization.

On the way down the stairs, Nick stopped to look at the brilliantly colored frogs populating the front stoop. Cassandra had told him a neighbor had illegally imported the frogs, nearly two-hundred, and had released them. The reason for his behavior was unclear; it was more than five years ago and the frogs had prospered.

Much of the fauna imported to Hawaii, legally or illegally, left their mark on the islands. In 1883, the Pacific Sugar Mill brought seventy-two mongooses from Jamaica to the Island of Hawaii to control rats in their sugarcane fields. Their offspring were shipped to other sugar plantations on Oahu, Maui, and Moloka'i. The plan failed, the mongoose being nocturnal and the rat diurnal. Mongeese decimated the population of the ground-laying *nēnē*, the Hawaiian goose and the *'alalā*, the Hawaiian crow and the *'u'au*, the petrel, a seabird. The state has been trying to control the invasive species ever since.

The one imported species that has kept its population in check is the wallaby. In 1919, a pair escaped from a private zoo in Kalihi Valley. The wallabies spread from Nu'uanu Valley above Downtown Honolulu to Halawa Valley, above the airport. In recent years, the colony of about 40 wallabies had returned to Kalihi Valley.

As Nick stepped over the frogs on his way to his car, he wondered what havoc they were wreaking on the ecosystem.

Chapter Eight

The next Sunday Nick had plans to sail on *Caprice*, Willie's forty foot sailing catamaran, which he moored on the south shore in Ke'ehi Lagoon near the airport. He had brought the boat from his dock at home in Kailua, on the windward side of Oahu, to have one of the engines serviced the following week.

The crew met at the boat at ten o'clock and set sail around eleven. The group included Willie, his current monogamous girlfriend Helena, her eight-year-old son Chad, Tina and Charlotte, two of Willie's friends attending graduate school at the university, and Nigel.

"Thanks for the rescue, Nick," Charlotte said.

"No problem, Charlotte," Nick replied.

"Another rescue? You're having quite a month," Willie chimed in, coming from the cabin.

Charlotte told the crew about Nick pulling her out of the way of the oncoming bus.

"A bus? All he did was save me from drowning," Willie said.

"Ah, I'm sure another boat behind us would've picked you up. We got to you first. Right, Nigel?" Nick asked.

"Right. And we still won the race," Nigel said.

Nick motored out of Ke'ehi Lagoon and into the Pacific. Willie rarely drove the boat, except for taking *Caprice* into the slip, which he did at ridiculous speed, jamming the engines into reverse before the boat careened into the dock. He preferred to lounge in the stateroom with a book. In fact, Willie was rarely without a book. That day's reading material was *The Crying of Lot 49* by Thomas Pynchon.

When Nick asked Willie if he liked the book, Willie looked at the cover and said, "I can't decide if this is actually a post-modernist work or a play on post-modernist works. Either way, it's some weird stuff."

Once out of the channel, Nick turned into the wind toward Diamond Head, and the others raised the mainsail and unfurled the jib. He pointed the boat to fill the sails and killed the engine. A collective sigh emanated from the crew. There is hardly a way to describe the beauty of the silence after turning off a rumbling diesel and moving only under the power of the wind, comfortably enveloped in the quiet.

The sea was flat and the wind blew just enough to give the boat forward speed. It wasn't long before only Helena was left on the boat. For safety, they dragged six lines trailing floats before the rest of the crew jumped overboard. The boat moved at half a knot; the water was the perfect temperature, and the lack of engine noise made for a silent swim a mile offshore. They saw the bottom in sixty feet of water. After an idyllic forty-five minutes, they climbed back into the boat and had a lunch of bread, cheese, avocados, grapes, oranges, and water. Tina opened a bag and pulled out a hand of bananas.

"Bananas? Who brought bananas?" Willie yelled, seeing them on the hatch cover. "Bananas are bad luck on a boat."

"Oh. I didn't know," Tina said.

Willie headed below, grumbling about bananas as he went.

"Why are bananas bad luck on a boat?" Chad asked.

"Yeah, why are bananas bad luck on a boat?" Nigel asked.

They both turned to Nick for an answer. Nick thought about everything he had read regarding bananas and seafaring. "From what I have read and heard, bananas give off ethylene gas, which causes other fruit on board to ripen quickly and would cause them to spoil before they reached their destination. Obviously, that's bad for the owner of the boat shipping the bananas. Also, when the bananas ripen too quickly, they ferment and produce alcohol, which of course is flammable and not a great idea on a wooden vessel."

Nick took an orange off of the hatch cover and peeled it.

"Another thought is because boats shipping bananas were hurrying to their destinations before they spoiled, so fishermen on board could not catch many fish on the voyage. Some fishermen thought that the smell of bananas was a natural fish repellent."

"Are they? Are bananas a natural fish repellent?" Chad asked.

"Who knows? Sailors are a notoriously superstitious lot," Nigel said.

"Also, spiders." Nick added. "In the 1600s and 1700s there were lots of merchants trading bananas. Spiders would come on board with the bananas and lay eggs, which would later hatch. Some spiders were venomous, and medicine not being the way it is today, occasionally a sailor would die from a spider bite." Nick said, taking a bite of orange.

"And banana peels are very slippery," Chad said.

"Yes, and banana peels are very slippery," Nick agreed.

They sat back, lounging in the cockpit, sated and relaxed. Nick didn't know what it was about boats that made people randy. Maybe it is, as they say, the motion of the ocean. At any rate, the discussion started tamely enough.

"How did your tennis game with the ex girlfriend go?" Nick asked.

"Jeanette destroyed me, but I enjoyed dinner after the game," Nigel replied.

"Well, she *does* teach tennis," Nick said, turning the wheel to keep the sails filled.

"Yes, I've become a much better player since we met. I'm glad we could stay friends," Nigel said, reaching for a banana, peeling it, and taking a bite. "There's nothing like pain to offset the pleasure," he added.

"Pain and pleasure are mixed up in a lot of people's minds, anyway," Tina added.

"It's a normal human reaction," said Charlotte, joining the fray.

"Getting tied up and spanked by your lover is a normal human reaction?" Tina blurted. Nigel and Nick exchanged amused glances.

"Who said anything about tying anyone up and spanking anyone?" Charlotte demanded.

"Excuse me. Could we perhaps put parameters on this conversation?" Nick asked, gesturing to Chad. He had been sitting in the corner of the cockpit.

"Uh," Tina grunted, turning red in the face.

They all turned to look.

Chad's eyes were like saucers.

"Ready to come about?" Nick asked the crew. The tacking metaphor seemed appropriate.

He pulled in the mainsheet, turned the boat to starboard, and released the sheet again. Nigel manned the foresail as they headed back through the channel to the lagoon. Nick tuned the boat to sail upwind, catching every ounce of wind to avoid tacking in the channel and disrupting the traffic.

"Wow, what's that?" Chad asked, pointing down the channel.

"Where did that come from? It wasn't there a second ago," Nick asked.

"What is it? It looks like a tornado," Charlotte said.

"It kind of is. It's a waterspout," Nick said, looking around. It was heading up the channel, staying to the starboard side. There wasn't the room or time to get away from it. It would be right on top of the boat if he moved, and Nick had no choice but to hold his course. He gave the mainsheet a tug and hoped the wind didn't shift. Nick eyed the lee shore of the narrow channel with its sharp, straight edges visible beneath the clear water where coral had been blasted and cut.

As the boat and the waterspout closed their gap, they heard the whoosh. Nick knew waterspouts can spin at nearly 100 miles an hour.

"Everyone hold tight to a lifeline or stanchion," he called. They moved to a safe position. Chad had his arms and legs wrapped around the base of the mast. The waterspout picked up speed as it approached the boat. Nick edged *Caprice* as close as he dared to the channel wall. Nigel reached out to feel the edge of the wind. They were mesmerized as the waterspout moved past the beam of *Caprice* and continued up the channel.

"That was cool," Chad said.

"Only because it missed us," Nick said. "Nigel, let's drop the sails."

Nick leaned down to the base of the lazarette and started the engine. He engaged the drive and pushed forward on the throttle. The boat sped up, then died, and fell silent again.

"Now what?" Nick asked no-one in particular.

Willie, having missed the entire waterspout event, came on deck. "Why did you kill the engine?" he asked.

"I didn't," Nick said, looking down at the gauges and then over the transom. "Uh, oh. I see the problem. There's a line overboard. We must have missed taking one in after we swam. I thought we got them all."

"Wrapped around the prop?" Willie asked.

"I'm afraid so," Nick said.

"Too bad the other engine is out of commission," Willie said.

Nick took off his shirt. "Take the wheel and I'll go down and clear the line."

"No, I'll go." Willie took a dive knife and a dive mask from a hatch and jumped off the stern.

"I want a swim anyway," Willie said from the water, then took a breath and dove. Nick once again eyed the lee shore. The wind had shifted and dropped. Nick made a quick decision. "Nigel, get the jib back out and raise the mainsail. Chad, can you please get the boat pole and hand it to Nigel when he's done with the sails. Quickly please, Chad."

Nick turned the wheel away from the channel wall and let out the limp sails. The wind was not strong enough to turn the boat. They had thirty feet to go before they hit the channel wall, but their drift was slow. Nick saw Willie's bubbles break the surface. He looked to starboard. Nigel, pole in hand and ready to push off, was amidships with Chad. They nervously watched the approaching channel wall.

"Are we going to hit?" Charlotte asked.

"No," Nick said. "We are not going to hit. How's he doing, Helena?"

Helena sat on the transom deck, feet in the water, leaning forward.

"I can't tell."

Nick saw the troubled line move. He reached down and turned the key to ON.

"Helena, we will only have a few seconds. Can you get ready on the starter? I want to keep my hands on the controls."

"Okay."

Nick knew it would be close.

A bubble came from the stern, and Willie's head broke the surface.

"Hurry, Willie." Nick said, putting the engine in neutral.

Willie hauled himself onto the transom deck. "I'm clear of the prop."

"Go, Helena," Nick said. Helena pushed the starter and the engine coughed, sputtered. She pushed the starter again and the engine caught. Nick dropped the lever into reverse, turned the wheel, and pushed the throttle forward. The prop cavitated, the water in the stern bubbled and frothed, and the boat pulled back away from the shore. When they were twenty feet from the edge, Nick retarded the throttle. A collective sigh of relief emanated from the crew.

Nigel made his way back to the cockpit. "Rather close, Nick, less than a meter."

"Flippin' bananas!" Willie yelled from the transom.

Chapter Nine

A few days later, Nick had *Icarus* towed to the Kewalo Basin to have her hauled out. A small crowd of locals and tourists watched as Sam supervised the slings being slid under the bow and stern. He stopped his helper occasionally and moved a sling or made an adjustment. They hoisted the boat out of the water and craned it to the boatyard to cradle it on blocks.

It always amazed Nick how big a fifty-seven foot boat looked on land. He made a thorough inspection of the craft and pulled the keel bolt and inspected it for rot and deterioration. The naval bronze bolt looked fine, and Nick took comfort in the fact the keel would not fall off the boat and sink to the bottom of the Pacific.

Nick found the rest of *Icarus* to be in fine shape. The years and upkeep had been kind to the boat, but it was time to sand, re-caulk the seams, paint, and replace or update the through-hull fittings and, at Willie's suggestion, put in a second, back-up bilge pump.

By the afternoon, Sam's team had hoisted the old Detroit Diesel engine from its compartment. A painstakingly slow process, Nick oversaw every aspect. It was a lot of mass to be moving in a small area. With the engine removed, Nick crawled into the engine bay to inspect it.

The space, grimy and ugly, showed the original paint where the engine had prevented access. The area was big enough for Nick to sit upright. He felt around for soft spots in the wood and found no sign of water intrusion. He would clean it up and paint it a gloss white, a sure way to spot leaks.

As he turned to crawl from the space, he spied a brown bottle wedged in by the cooling intake. Nick reached in and pulled it free. He read the label. It was a bottle of Bay Rum, his grandfather's favorite aftershave. He figured it had been there since the engine was installed. He opened the bottle and took a delicate sniff. The smell immediately brought back memories of his grandfather: Sunday dinners with his grandparents after a sail, his grandfather reading to Nick after dinner, usually something of a nautical nature.

Nick shook some of the aftershave on to his palm and spread it on his face.

Chapter Ten

"What are you working on, Nick?" Keoni asked, passing down Nick's daypack from the lifeguard tower.

"I'm writing a business plan for a startup company."

"What are they starting up?"

"Digital graphics, software, the normal start-up thing."

"There's a lot of that going on in Hawaii."

Nick sat at his usual spot in the shade on San Souci Beach. He had come out of the water from a swim and as he spread out his towel, a blue and gold macaw flew by, landing in a palm tree to his right. There was a flock of colorful parrots that lived in the trees on the beach. Some had been let loose by their owners, some had escaped from the zoo and nature parks, and some, Nick assumed, had grown tired of posing for photographs with tourists in Waikiki.

Nick sat down, took his laptop out of his daypack, and got to work. Blaine had sent him enough information for him to get started on the business plan.

Using his mobile phone for an internet connection, Nick got online to research the market and competitors. Blaine had given him a rough outline of his expected sales. The estimates were, in Nick's opinion, optimistic.

Hours later, with the sun lower in the sky and his laptop battery drained, he packed up and headed to his car. The next morning he started the process again. His days were defined for a while: get up, eat, go to the boatyard and work on the boat in the cooler morning, clean up, exercise, lunch, go for a swim, work on the business plan, and dinner. It was a good life. His office was a beach and his schedule was his own.

To save money, Nick did much of the work on *Icarus*. Once he started, he saw how big a job it was and hired a university student to help him prepare the hull for painting. Together they scraped barnacles, re-caulked, filled seams, and sanded. Then came the primer and paint.

One morning Willie came down to help him cut a hole for the additional bilge pump. Nick had a sick feeling drilling a hole in the hull—it seemed against the nature of seamanship.

"Man, the air is foul today," Willie said, coughing into his sleeve.

"It's blowing Kona's," Nick said.

The volcano on the Big Island was active, and the trade winds had died down. It was hot and a slight breeze from Kona carried sulfur dioxide from the volcano, which mixed with water vapor and sunlight. The resulting volcanic smog, or *vog*, had blanketed Oahu. There would be people complaining of itchy eyes and sinus headaches for a day or two.

After the morning of vog, Nick and Willie scouted the marine supply stores and found an air conditioner that would fit perfectly in the mid-deck hatch of *Icarus*. It would be a fresh addition to the boat, and something he hadn't needed when

Icarus was docked in the San Francisco Bay. Living aboard in Honolulu, it became a necessity during much of the year. It would also dehumidify the boat, keeping mold and mildew in check.

Nick and Willie, after adding the new bilge pump, installed a solar panel and wind turbine on *Icarus*. When he was sailing offshore, the sun and the wind would keep the batteries topped off without having to run the engine.

"Hello, Nick," Sam called from the foot of the ladder leaning against the transom. "Permission to come aboard?"

"Come on up, Sam."

Sam climbed the ladder and sat down in the shade of the dodger. For a moment he watched Nick work at replacing a bent turnbuckle.

"I have bad news, I'm afraid," Sam started.

Nick finished removing the old turnbuckle and set it on the hatch cover. He turned to Sam. "What's up?"

"The arrival of your new engine is delayed. I was told they shipped it the day I ordered it and it would be here five days later. But now I am told that is not the case."

"When will it arrive?"

"The order didn't make it into their system, so we are starting from scratch. But now it's back ordered. I called around to other suppliers, but they say the same thing; it's back ordered."

"Where does that leave us?"

"I'm sorry, but it will be a couple of weeks before we will see your engine."

"That's too bad. I painted the engine compartment and the prep work is done," Nick gestured to the empty space below them. "I'm ready to install it now."

"I'm sorry about the mixup. I won't charge you for the extra shore time, but I have to move your boat to the side of the yard. A seventy-footer is coming in and I need the room."

"No problem. Thanks for the break. This has cost me a lot more than I anticipated."

"It's common with the bigger, older wooden boats," Sam said.

After Sam left him alone on *Icarus*, Nick knew he made the right decision to rent the room in Manoa Valley for a month.

Chapter Eleven

I n two weeks, Nick had finished the narrative portion of the business plan. He had been meeting with Blaine a few times a week to clarify elements of the plan, always at *Little Village Noodle House*. Nick left for their meetings earlier each time, trying to arrive before Blaine had ordered and started eating. He never got there ahead of Blaine and gave up after the third try.

At each meeting, Blaine became increasingly excited with Nick's process. One day at the restaurant, Blaine greeted him with "I have investors lined up to read your plan when you have it finished. They are eager to invest." Blaine spoke to Nick between bites of taro duck, part of which again ended up on his shirt.

"They must have a lot of faith in you. I'm still a couple of weeks from completion. The financials will take me longer than the narrative."

"That's cool. They'll be ready when you are."

Nick was taken aback. He hadn't completed the plan and Blaine had already found investors?

After lunch, Nick walked around Chinatown, stopping along the way to look in the shop windows. He saw an herbalist with a wall of wooden drawers, an antique store stuck in the 1950s, and, a rare find, a travel agency. Then, on Smith Street, he came upon a treasure, *Old Ironside Tattoo*, once *Sailor Jerry's Tattoo Shop*. Norman Keith Collins, known as *Sailor Jerry*, also known as *Old Ironside* was a tattoo artist, famous in World War II. He was also a licensed skipper, saxophonist, and dance band leader. *Sailor Jerry Rum* bears his name.

Nick walked past the yellow door with a round brass port-hole window and peered in. A man on a cot lay passively while a tattooist plied his needle. Prints of sample tattoos covered the walls, a mix of modern and old-fashioned—anchors and line, schooners, dragons, and pin-up girls. Nick peered in the window and thought if he were to get a tattoo, this is the place to do it, something matching the age and era of *Icarus*.

After a while, he continued down the street. Through a window he saw the barber, a woman, alone in the small shop, reading a Chinese language magazine. Nick saw his reflection in the glass.

He needed a haircut.

He entered the shop and the barber jumped up and motioned to the chair closest to the window. Once seated, Nick took in the shop as the barber readied her tools. It was a simple place, organized and clean. A single framed rice paper with the image of a flowering plum blossom branch adorned the wall. In the corner, a tall Chinese vase held living bamboo shoots. In another corner, joss sticks burned in a Buddhist shrine, filling the shop with a woody scent.

The barber gestured to Nick, pantomiming cutting his hair, holding her fingers apart and making scissoring motions with her other hand.

Nick nodded.

What followed was the most intricate, detailed, and accurate haircut he had ever received. For much of his life, Nick had gone to the same barbershop as his father had in his hometown of San Francisco. Nick watched the concentration of the barber in the mirror; the woman was an artist. She spun his chair so he faced the window. Nick saw Blaine across the street, in an animated conversation with a tall thin man in an ill-fitting, rumpled gray three-piece suit. The man had a beat-up black briefcase, not unlike the one Nick's grandfather had carried. *I wonder what became of that case?*

The man pointed down to Blaine. It was clear by the body language he was the one, not Blaine, who held the power, the one in control. Nick peered through the window and watched them closely. Blaine nodded his head, and the tall, thin man turned and walked away. There was no shaking of hands.

That's interesting. Nick looked down at the floor. The barber was wearing crepe sole shoes that caught and held the hair.

She had fuzzy, hairy shoes.

Chapter Twelve

Nick had been working on the boat and writing the business plan. It was a good balance and he made progress.

With the hull work done on *Icarus*, Nick kept the original paint scheme, a dark blue hull with a sharp red stripe. He restored the brightwork to its former glory—the brass polished and the teak sanded and varnished. Nick set aside the morning to work on the running rigging—the moving lines controlling the sails. The following day he worked on the standing rigging, holding the two masts in place. After that, he pulled the twelve sails off the boat to inspect and repair any weak spots. He sat in the shade of the boat, using a sailor's palm to sew rips in the sails. With the sails out of the forepeak, he scrubbed and cleaned the interior. He took off the cushion covers and had them professionally cleaned.

As for the business plan, the afternoons of sitting on the beach with his laptop had produced a solid document. He felt if Blaine's contacts were as good as he touted; the business had a good chance of succeeding, even with his inflated revenue projections. Of course, hiring the right people would have much to do with the company's success.

At their next lunch meeting, Nick presented Blaine with the final plan, which he read at the table.

Blaine was ecstatic and the papers were splattered with taro duck sauce by the end of the meal.

That evening at the house in Manoa Valley, Nick made a dinner salad of Manoa lettuce and other locally grown vegetables. To Nick, it was worth rising early to go to the local farmers' market. The produce was fresher than what was in the grocery stores. As he took out the rubbish, he saw a wondrous sight. Still with wings, termites buzzed about a streetlight. Below them buffos, Texas-sized toads, up to ten inches long before they stretched out, also swarmed. From up and down the street they came to dine. Nick counted twenty-two from the front porch. The buffos gorged themselves, tongues flicking hither and yon, not putting a dent in the flying termite population.

He retrieved a beach chair from his car and sat on the patch of grass to watch the show. A while later he heard a voice beside him ask, "Hi, I'm your neighbor, Christine. Can I join you?"

She carried a lawn chair and two open bottles of beer.

"Please do. I'm Nick." She handed him a beer and set up her chair. They took sips, the cold beverage refreshing on the balmy night.

"Thanks. This hits the spot," Nick said.

They sat in silence, viewing the spectacle before them with an awed amazement. It was carnage in the animal kingdom.

"Uh, oh."

"What's wrong?" Nick asked.

"Ichabod, my cat. He's stalking a buffo."

The cat was across the street and almost on the toad. Nick knew he couldn't get to the cat before it attacked.

"This should be interesting," Nick said.

"Poor buffo!" Christine said.

"Poor cat!"

"What do you mean? I'm sure a toad is no match for Ichabod."

"Perhaps. Let's watch."

The cat pounced, landing astride a large specimen. He turned his head to bite the toad. The buffo held his ground.

"See, Ikky's got it," Christine narrated, "He's pretty sure of himself."

"The toad doesn't look concerned. I think it's more sure of himself," Nick said.

The cat jumped backwards, spitting and meowing.

"What just happened?" Christine asked.

"Those toads secrete a slime which tastes really foul. It's a built in defense," Nick replied.

"No kidding."

"It's reported to be a hallucinogen if one gets enough licks in."

"No kidding."

Ichabod, still meowing, coughed, spit, and wiped its paw on its mouth, eyeing the toad warily.

A slight rain began to fall, and the buffos made their way back to the bushes. Christine and Nick stood with the lawn chairs above their heads, watching them depart.

"Show's over," Nick said. "Thanks again for the beer."

"I'd better check on my cat."

Ichabod scampered about in the rain, hopping like a kangaroo.

"It looks as though the drugs are taking effect," she said, heading to the feline.

Chapter Thirteen

That following evening when Nick arrived at the house in Manoa Valley, Persie was putting her dishes in the dishwasher.

While Nick made a salad, Persie prattled on from non sequitur to non sequitur, telling him she worked at an art gallery in town, liked to go to the beach, grew up in the Midwest, had a boyfriend she broke up with and how when she ovulated she felt compelled to track him down and sleep with him. Nick, alternatively intrigued and amused, was sure he had met no one like her. He sat at the table to eat. Persie moved to the living room and turned on a teenage drama series.

Zeke appeared on top of the chair opposite him. Nick ate while the lizard watched. He finished his salad and took the dish to the sink, rinsed the bowl and opened the dishwasher. Persie had filled the entire bottom rack of the dishwasher with two bowls and a plate. Nick considered it a special form of brilliance, an unsolvable puzzle, yet solved, and right in front of him. He shook his head and rearranged the dishes to make room for his bowl.

Persie came up behind him. "There's a lizard on the dining chair."

"Oh, that's Zeke. He kind of follows me around."

"Okaaaay," she said, looking between Nick and the lizard.

Nick picked up a Buddha statue next to the sink. The back was open and there was a small hole in the belly.

"That's where the straw goes," Persie volunteered.

"The straw?"

"Yeah, I got it at a bar in Waikiki. When you order a mai tai, they give it to you in the Buddha glass. You sip the drink out of a straw in his belly."

Nick set the statue back down.

"I wonder what the Buddhists would think of that."

"What do you mean?"

"I mean I'm sure they would find it sacrilegious."

"How can it be sacrilegious?" she asked.

"What if that were a statue of Jesus and you were sucking liquor from his belly button?"

"It's not the same thing," she scoffed, walking back and plopping down in front of the television.

Nick was sure it was "the same thing". When he bought his Triumph from a man named Larry, a ribbon of gold Chinese characters on orange silk hung from the rear-view mirror.

"Tell me about the ribbon," Nick asked.

"The ribbon is a blessing. My father gave it to me when I bought the car," Larry said. "My mother insisted."

"That's nice," Nick said.

"My father's a monk at the buddhist temple."

"I wasn't aware Buddhist monks married."

"In Japan, Taiwan, and Korea, some monks can marry. My father's from Taiwan. My mother's American."

Nick took the ribbon in his hand, turned it over, examined it.

"I can remove it if you wish," Larry said.

"I'll tell you what. I'll buy the car, but on one condition."

Larry eyed Nick. "What condition is that?"

"That you respectfully ask your father to reapply the blessing for me."

Larry let out a laugh. "You bet. He's home now." He removed the ribbon from the mirror and took it in the house.

While he waited, Nick continued examining the car. He started and revved the engine. On his test drive he was surprised at its performance.

"When I bought it, I found it to be underpowered, so I put in a special camshaft, exhaust, carburetors, and ignition system. It runs great," Larry had told him.

It was in good shape for its age, but even with Larry's modifications Nick knew he was crazy to buy such an unreliable car. He figured being on an island it couldn't strand him too far from help or home. *Perhaps the blessing will help*, he mused.

Larry came back with the ribbon.

"My father wants to meet you. He'll be out in a second."

A large, smiling man wearing a yellow robe came from the house. He took the orange ribbon and hung it on the rear-view mirror, chanting as he did.

When he finished, he took a red string from the pocket of his robe. Larry handed his father a charm, a seated Buddha. The monk slid the charm on the red string and tied it on Nick's left wrist. "Promise yourself you will not have negative actions or negative thoughts of others," he said.

"I try to do that now," Nick replied.

The monk nodded.

"Good. Negative thoughts will interfere with your desire for protection and fulfillment."

He made seven simple knots. Larry handed his father a knife with which he trimmed off the extra length. The monk spoke a prayer while he held Nick's wrist.

"It is a prayer of blessing and protection," he said. "The red string is a reminder of the strength of your faith and will help you perpetuate focus and healing. The Buddha charm will remind you to be more Buddha-like throughout the day, and to be more kind and patient. It will help you cultivate thoughts of nonviolence and peace. The symbol is sacred, as is any representation of the Buddha."

Nick put his hands together over his heart and bowed to the monk, and then to Larry.

Both father and son threw back their heads in laughter.

Chapter Fourteen

The next morning, Nick's mobile phone rang.

"I found investors for the company." Blaine used his conspiratorial voice in delivering the message.

"That's great." Nick found himself unintentionally mimicking Blaine's vocal pattern.

"I want you to come work for me. I need a Chief Operating Officer and I want you to be a member of the Board of Directors."

It was a lot to take in. Blaine's salesmanship impressed Nick —from plan to funding in two weeks.

"You said you don't want stock, but I'll offer it to you anyway, with a nice salary." Blaine mentioned a figure.

Nick shook his head in disbelief. It was a mainland-level executive start-up Silicon Valley salary. In Hawaii, it was unheard of. With the work on *Icarus* costing him much of his savings, he needed the additional income.

He accepted the offer.

"What do you say we meet and talk it over face-to-face?"

"Tomorrow at *Little Village*?"

"I'll meet you there at our usual time."

"Cool. I'll order the taro duck."

Nick wondered if Blaine owned the restaurant.

The next day, as Nick drove away from *Little Village*, he considered the prospect. The job would be a novel experience, and who knows where it could lead?

He stopped at his post office box to retrieve his mail and post a letter to his friend Francois in Tahiti.

"I'd like to send this letter, please," he said, handing the envelope to a young woman behind the counter.

She grasped the red, white and blue airmail envelope and inspected it. On the left side there was a circle with the words "Air Mail, *Par Avion,* and *Correo Aereo*." She took a pen and crossed out the non-English words.

Nick didn't ask for an explanation. Why ruin the moment?

Chapter Fifteen

B etween writing the business plan, sailing, and working on *Icarus*, Nick spent few daylight hours at the house in Manoa Valley. Persie was usually there in the evenings when he arrived; Casandra was on a sojourn on the mainland. Persie had parked herself in front of the television, eating a sandwich and watching her teen drama series when Nick walked into the room that evening.

Having found no sharp knife in the kitchen, Nick had brought his favorite knife from *Icarus*. It was a gift from a Japanese friend, custom made of ceramic and housed in a carved wood box. It was insanely expensive.

He had left the knife in its box on the kitchen counter. When he returned home that night, he showered and headed to the kitchen to make dinner.

He opened the knife box and let out a surprised "Aghhh."

The tip of the knife was broken off.

"What happened to my knife?" he asked Persie.

"Oh, I couldn't find the can opener for the tuna, so I used the knife in the box on the counter. The tip broke. Sorry." She turned back to the television.

Nick examined the knife. Not only was the tip missing, the blade was chipped and beyond repair. It was useless. Nick put it back in the exquisitely carved box.

"I dropped a tuna can into the sink drain and couldn't get it out," Persie said from the couch.

Nick looked into the sink where Persie had wedged the can in the drain. He took the knife from the box and used it to pry it out. He dropped the knife and the can into the rubbish bin. The last few years had taught him not to get attached to things, although he kept the box. It was perfect for his drawing pencils.

Later that night reading in his room, he thought about his roommate. Persie reminded him of the Meg Ryan character from the movie *Joe Versus the Volcano*. Tom Hanks' character called her a *flibbertigibbet*.

From then on, that's how Nick saw her.

Zeke climbed onto his bedside table. "Oh, hello Zeke. I'll think of her as 'Flibby' for short. What do you think, Zeke?"

A knock on the door interrupted their discussion.

"Yes?"

Flibby opened the door and poked her head in. "I want to say sorry again about the knife." She pointed to Zeke on the bedside table. "Hey, he does follow you around. That's weird," she said and then closed the door.

Chapter Sixteen

The next day the weather changed abruptly, not uncommon in the tropics. It was one of those hot, humid, rain-filled fall days. The Ewa Plain had received two inches of rain in the last hour, and the storm swept east into Honolulu.

Nick planned to meet Joe, a client he had worked with a few months prior, for dinner and drinks at a restaurant on the waterfront. He knew the high humidity would cause trouble with his car. Lucas, the maker of the electrical systems of British vehicles, was referred to by some owners of British cars as *Lucas, The Prince of Darkness*.

Sure enough, the turn signals slowed down and the wiper blades moved sluggishly across the windscreen. Nick had tried to remedy the problem many times to no avail. When the weather got humid, the old Triumph did not like it. He could relate. Inside, the car felt like a sauna.

On the way to his appointment, a deluge hit and the sky filled with lightning flashes. The car responded as if frightened. It leapt and bucked, the engine cutting in and out. Water streamed through where the windshield connected to the top, flowing down across the steering wheel and onto Nick's lap. Leaks sprang from elsewhere. Water poured onto his legs. Nearing his destination, he got into the line for valet parking. As he did, the wipers stopped in the vertical position, blades up, saluting the world.

The car seat was wet, as was his own.

"It's really wet in here," Nick told the valet as he climbed out of the car. "Are you sure you don't want me to park it?"

"No problem. I'll take it," he said, climbing in and sitting down. "Hey, it's soaking in here," he barked from the driver's seat.

Nick made his way to the restaurant, ducking under awnings to stay dry. There was nowhere to walk to be away from relentless rain or inch-deep pools of water. He made it to the bar and waited. Joe was running late as he, too, drove an English car, an MG.

"I'm soaked," Joe said, his aloha shirt plastered to his body, hair dripping. He shook his head like a poodle, spraying the bar and neighboring drinkers. One patron held his hand out as if he were feeling for rain.

"You too?" Nick asked, motioning to the bartender.

"And Lucas is in fine form tonight. There were sparks shooting out of my speedometer."

"That's a new one."

They ordered drinks and *pupus* and talked and ate and drank. They had been working on Joe's underwater navigation system. Nick had written the marketing plan, and Joe wanted to discuss a few additions Nick had made. It was a productive meeting punctuated by thunder and lightning. At nine-thirty, they had finished their discussions and sat back in their chairs, full and content. The wind calmed and the rain had stopped.

"What do you think?" Nick asked.

"I'm going to make a run for it."

"Let's go," Nick said, getting up and tossing down a tip.

They made their way to the cars, handing the valet their tickets. The valet drove up in Joe's car and he climbed in.

"Bon chance," Nick called.

"Aloha," Joe responded as he roared off with a wave.

Nick climbed into his car. The electrical system was still confused, the wipers still pointed skyward, occluding the view through the window. Nick looked up at the clear sky and unlatched the top to push it back and started his drive home. The car stuttered again and Nick sped up. He was going thirty-five when he came over a rise and saw the road flooded in front of him. He hit it at speed and the Triumph dove, not unlike a submarine, into the water. As if in slow motion, Nick watched the wave begin at the front of the hood and travel toward him. When the water hit the windshield, it traveled up and crested the top, dumping buckets of water onto his head. He gasped and the car groaned and faltered, as if saying, "No more! I can take no more!"

The car plowed through the water, and Nick came to a stoplight at the end of the lake. He pushed in the clutch and revved the engine to keep it from dying. He laughed at the absurdity of it. A truck came up beside him at the stop.

"Hey Brah, we saw it. You okay?" the passenger asked.

"Yes, but I don't need to take a shower tonight," Nick laughed.

"Crazy *haole*," the driver commented, and pulled away.

Keeping Nick's little black car on the road dictated constant maintenance. The submarine escapade punctuated the need, and he had ordered a new convertible top, which arrived the following week.

Nick enlisted Nigel, who was blessed with an obscene degree of patience. Being a live-aboard sailor, he was handy with tools, and spoke the native British tongue of Nick's car.

"Listen to this," Nick said, reading instructions that came with the new top. "Find a nice, warm day, a patient friend, and a couple of large bottles of beer."

"Where did you get the top?" Nigel asked.

"It came direct from England."

"Cheeky buggers. Did you buy the beer?"

Nick lifted a cooler from the passenger seat and opened it to show Nigel. "I did."

The tropical climate cooperated with the need for a nice warm day, and the timing was perfect. Nick had to wait for the paint to cure on *Icarus*.

The instructions should have added

Gather every tool you own and assemble them beside the car.

The process required cutting metal, plastic, and cloth. Nick and Nigel glued, bolted, sewed, melted, sanded, painted, drilled, and taped. Four hours later, Nick had a dry cocoon of an interior and a slight sunburn.

"When you find another girl, you will have to get rid of this car," Nigel commented, wiping his hands.

"How do you figure?" Nick asked.

"You have a propensity for dating high-maintenance women, correct?"

"If by 'high-maintenance' you mean, complicated, intelligent, spirited women who tend to be demanding, then yes."

"The way I figure it, you have a high-maintenance car and you have a boat, which by definition is high-maintenance. I don't see how you have time for this car, your boat, and the high maintenance woman. And you will never get rid of that boat."

Chapter Seventeen

The following Friday, Nigel and Nick sat in the bar at the Waikiki Yacht Club. They had returned from the Friday night race and were waiting for Willie, who called to say he was nearby and going to drop in.

"Are you going to do race week?" Nigel asked. He was referring to the around-the-islands race which culminated on the Labor Day holiday with a seventy-eight mile downwind run from Maui to Honolulu.

"I'd like to. I'll probably fly to Maui and jump on board for the Lahaina return. I can get us on *Mystic Dancer*. You want to come along?" Nigel asked, taking a sip of whisky.

"How's the captain?" Nick asked.

"He's calm. Not the bellowing type. He's a retired Navy Commander."

Willie walked up. "You guys talking about Lahaina?"

"We're trying to figure what to do," Nigel said.

"Why don't we do it on *Caprice*?" Willie asked, munching on a *malasada* from Leonard's Bakery. "The return only. I don't want to do the whole race. Racing is for idiots. The return is more like an eight-hour downwind party."

"That's more relaxing than being on most boats I can think of," Nick said.

"And faster," Nigel added. "*Caprice* can really get out of its own way."

Nick ordered Willie a Steinlager and they put their heads together to plan the trip.

"Why don't we sail to Moloka'i the weekend before the race, overnight at my family's place, and then continue on to Lahaina?" Willie took a sip of beer. "I'll stay on the boat and you guys can fly back for the workweek. Then you can get back to Maui the following weekend before the race. Lahaina is a lot of fun on race weekend."

They agreed it was a good idea and worked together to sort out the details.

Chapter Eighteen

Nick worked on *Icarus* after his lunch meeting with Blaine, and it was dark when he drove his Triumph toward Manoa Valley. As he drove up Punahou Street, the scent of night-blooming cereus filled the air. Nick parked his car beside the rock wall of Punahou School and got out. The plant, which blooms only one night a year, had dozens of white flowers draped on the wall. Nick stood back and took in the scent of the seven-inch wide blossoms.

By the time he got back into the car, three more cars had parked behind him to take in the sight and smell.

Nick walked into a dramatic scene when he got back at the house. Cassandra had returned from her mainland trip and Flibby, in a state of panic, paced the living room, wringing her hands, speaking in more non sequiturs.

Flibberish, Nick thought. *She's speaking Flibberish.*

"What's going on?" Nick asked, setting his day pack on the floor of his bedroom.

"Cassie got back from her trip to the mainland."

"You wanted her to stay on the mainland?" Nick asked. She traversed the room a few more times. Nick took a seat on the couch and watched her pace.

"No. On her trip she got together with Tim, a friend of ours from college."

Nick sat and waited for her to go on. After a few more laps around the room she continued.

"I've got to get out of here; I need to find a new place to live," she said.

Nick waited as she completed four more laps.

"Tim and I kinda hooked up when we were in school together. Cassie doesn't know about it."

"Kind of hooked up?"

Flibby did another three laps.

"He's coming to stay with us in a few weeks. I've got to get out of here. I've got to find another place to live."

She spun around and aimed for her bedroom, leaving him in silence.

It's a good thing Icarus is nearly ready to go back in the water, Nick thought.

Chapter Nineteen

"I 'm in town. You want to grab dinner?" Willie asked when Nick answered his phone.

"Sure."

"Where are you?"

"I'm at the house in Manoa."

"I'll swing by and pick you up."

Half an hour later Nick was riding in Willie's 1980s white Cadillac.

"Where did you get this beast of a land barge and why are you driving it?" Nick asked.

"Isn't it great? I love this tank. A guy in my neighborhood was selling it and I had to have it."

Nick looked down at his feet and through the rusted holes in the floorboards. "Is this thing even safe? I can see the road going by."

"So far," Willie said, patting the dashboard. The light turned green and the car behind them honked. "Hey, no one honks in Hawaii. Must be a tourist."

The car sped around them. Nick saw a barcode on the rear window. "Good call."

"I suppose Little Village is out of the question?"

"Please, no."

"Death by taro duck?"

"Something like that."

Willie piloted the car to an Indian restaurant on King Street and he and Nick sat outside at a picnic table.

"I love Indian food. You're the only person I know that ever wants to eat it," Willie said, taking a sip of Kingfisher Beer.

"This place is a real find. It's better than a lot of the Indian restaurants I've been to on the mainland," Nick said, taking a bite of vegetable korma.

"So how's it going with the new company?"

"I finished the business plan and gave it to Blaine Daniels early this week. He has already secured funding."

"He already has funding? I don't know much about start-up companies, but that seems fast."

"It is."

Nick filled Willie in on the drama at his home. When Willie dropped him off later, Nick invited him in to see the House. As they entered, they saw Cassandra in the kitchen preparing something with garlic for dinner. Classical piano played on the stereo.

"Man, that smells great. It's making me hungry," Willie said.

"Willie, we just came from dinner," Nick said.

"So?"

"Anyway, you've got to meet this guy, Tom," Nick whispered. "He has no personality, and it's as if he has no life force. I call him 'The Specter'. He'd make the perfect spy."

"Sounds interesting. When do I get to meet him?"

"He's right there." Nick motioned with his head. Tom stood with his back to them, flipping through a magazine. "Go introduce yourself."

Willie looked up at Tom standing not ten feet from him. He jumped. "Jeeze, where did he come from?"

"He's been standing there since we walked in."

"The guy is gray," Willie whispered.

Nick regarded Tom. He *was* gray. His shorts and t-shirt were gray, his hat was gray, his slippers were gray. His hair was a mousy brown.

"You're right, he is gray. Maybe *The Specter* is a spy," Nick whispered.

Willie shook his head "That guy gives me the creeps!"

Chapter Twenty

The next day Nick met with Blaine at an empty office space on Waialae Avenue in Kaimuki, an area untouched by much of the modernization occurring in Hawaii. Kaimuki had old shops and a boarded-up run-down theater, a couple of excellent restaurants, and a coffee shop at the top of the hill. The space Blaine found had two stories with a mezzanine and a view of Diamond Head and the building on the inside looked new.

They sorted out Nick's employment agreement and Blaine told him he had others in line as management and officers of the new corporation. After that, things moved quickly. Blaine called around the island and found a company that had gone out of business shortly after opening their doors. They had spent their capital on furnishing their office and had little money left to pay their employees. Nick had seen it many times during his start-up days in San Francisco. Blaine made a deal to buy the furniture for twenty cents on the dollar, including delivery.

Later that month, Nick sat at a nearly new desk with matching furniture in a freshly painted building. Like the others in the management suite, his desk had the latest new computer. It was an elegant layout with the directors' offices surrounding a conference room in the center of the hub. Blaine's office had a private entrance accessible from the back of the building. Nick's office had a window with a view of a park across the street and a peek of Diamond Head. At the entryway to the offices sat Betty, the administrative assistant who acted as the receptionist and gatekeeper.

Nick got to know the other officers, who all had interesting backgrounds. The board meetings were during lunch at one of the better restaurants in town. The company took care of the bill and the group ordered-up. The lunches were long, rambling affairs with lots of alcohol. Nick abstained from drinking at lunch and took on the role of designated driver of the company car—a Mercedes Benz.

During those lunches, he got acquainted with the others Blaine chose for board members and officers.

Ben, the Chief Financial Officer, played guitar and drove a cab between gigs before joining the company.

Claire, the Chief Marketing Officer, taught pilates and yoga and sang karaoke on the weekend.

Blaine, Ben, and Claire knew each other; making Nick the outsider.

Nick recognized the person Blaine chose for legal council. Darby Jurgis was tall, had stringy shoulder-length hair and bad teeth. Nick thought back to the discussion he saw Jurgis and Blaine having while he had his haircut in Chinatown. *Was it more of an argument?* Nick remembered Jurgis looking like the dominant party.

Jurgis worked out of his apartment and played the bass whenever he got a gig.

After spending time with the team, Nick wondered what he had gotten himself into.

Blaine came bounding into the offices one morning. "I received the sketches for our new company logo. A friend of mine is an award-winning graphics designer and he did it for me."

The management team and Betty assembled at the conference room table.

Blaine opened the envelope. "I haven't seen them yet." He pulled a sheet from the envelope and set it on the conference table. The team leaned forward, inspecting the pages.

They were speechless.

"That is hideous," Claire said, breaking the silence. "It looks like a Volkswagen Beetle being carried away by an enormous bird. What did you tell him our company did?"

"Huh," grunted Blaine.

"It's really bad. It's so bad he must have been trying to make it bad on purpose. Maybe it's a *thing*," Ben said, his fingers up in air quotes.

"That's it!" Blaine snapped his fingers. "The logo is so bad it's cool!" He examined the pages once again. "I love it!"

Nick turned to Blaine to see if he was joking.

"How much did you pay him to design it?" Ben asked.

"Fifteen grand and it's worth every penny." Blaine took the paper from the table, slid it into the envelope. "This is cool!" he said, walking out of the conference room.

Betty rolled her eyes, made a 'tch' sound, and followed Blaine.

"I guess we have a cool new logo," Nick said.

Ben shook his head. "I must be getting old. I'm not sure what 'cool' means anymore."

A Chief Operating Officer is second in command, and depending upon the relationship between the Chief Executive Officer and the Chief Operating Officer, it can mean many things. Many COOs run the day-to-day operations of the company, including staffing, overseeing finance, and marketing.

The CEO, on the other hand, is the public face of the company, courts investors, does long-term planning, and builds alliances.

For the first few weeks, Nick worked hard trying to get Blaine to agree to a definition of their working relationship. Blaine continued to be vague and noncommittal, and said things like, "We'll figure it out as we go along."

So Nick dug into developing the software teams, the digital graphics, and medical billing products. Despite Blaine saying, "It's software running on computers," they were different teams with different computers. The skill sets were different, and they didn't even overlap. The digital graphics team used off-the-shelf software with graphical interfaces while the medical team was writing software from scratch. In the modern world of computing, Nick found it much easier to find digital graphic teams than competent programmers, especially in Hawaii with few people from whom to choose.

Overweight, doughy, and sloppy, Blaine was strong in ideas, and he came up with a lot of them. As Nick built a development team, Blaine moved staff to another new project or idea he had come up with. He used any staff for anything—collecting his laundry or having the oil changed in his car. If he needed something done, anyone he came across in the hall could be sent on an errand.

Blaine had no focus nor short- or long-term planning. Perhaps that explained his four ex-wives.

One morning when Nick arrived at the office, he found someone sleeping under a desk in the programmers' room.

"There was someone sleeping under a desk in the programmers' room when I got in this morning," he told Blaine.

"That would be Kelvin," Blaine said.

"Kelvin, as in the temperature scale?"

"Yeah, his mother was a chemist and his father a physicist. It was the only name they could agree on. I think it's cool."

"Does Kelvin have a home?" Nick asked.

"Not yet. I flew him in to help us with the manual for the medical billing software."

"So, he's a technical writer, is he?"

"Not really. He needed a job and he's an old friend. You'll like him."

"How am I to use his talents?"

"We'll figure it out as we go along."

Claire came into the office at 10:30, her usual time after her yoga class. It made for short days with her taking a long lunch and leaving by 3:00. For the little time she spent there, her office was meticulously decorated. She had a custom cushion made for her desk chair. A credenza with a vase of anthuriums, ginger, and orchids took up one wall. There were motivational posters with pithy sayings and a shelf of self-help books.

That morning she trudged in, head down.

"What's the matter, Claire?" Nick felt obligated to ask. It was a common occurrence, and usually of the marital variety.

"John and I are getting a divorce."

"Wow, that is something. I'm sorry to hear that," Nick said.

"Of course, it's something. I found out he's been sleeping with his secretary. I suspected, but he fessed up this morning."

"It didn't sound like you two were happy," Nick offered.

"That's not the point. His secretary is a friend of mine. I can't believe it."

When Nick came into the office early the next morning, he saw a sculpture on a pedestal in the lobby. It was a figure, tall and spindly, with roughly sculpted limbs. It looked like a Giacometti. He assumed it was a reproduction.

He dropped his backpack in his office and made his way to the coffee counter. When he turned the corner in the hall, he heard banging noises coming from the programmers' room. He opened the door to investigate and found Kelvin beneath a desk with an intern under him.

"Do you mind closing the door on your way out?" the intern asked.

Nick backed out of the room and closed the door, and the noise resumed. Later that morning, Nick saw Blaine at the coffee counter.

"Kelvin was shagging an intern under a desk in the programmers' room when I got in this morning."

"Oh, yeah, that reminds me. I told him we would go shopping for a mattress today."

"Don't you think it's wrong for our, erm, older employees to be fraternizing with the interns? There *are* sexual harassment laws in Hawaii."

"Hey, it's consensual, isn't it? Besides, I introduced them."

The company grew at a furious clip, and while Nick tried to assemble a competent team, Blaine continued to bring in his own crowd of hangers-on, including Big Jack, who, true to his nickname, filled a doorway and weighed in at 310 pounds.

Big Jack wanted his own office. He didn't like the bright overhead lights; he didn't like the noise, and he didn't much like the people he worked with.

"There's no chance of getting your own office. We only have our large production areas," Nick told him.

"Well, that won't do," was Jack's reply.

Nick would have encouraged him to seek employment elsewhere, but he led the team for the medical billing software. He was the best programmer in the group, which he was fond of telling Nick.

After their meeting, Big Jack took matters into his own hands. He secured a corner desk in the programmers' room and went to work. He salvaged cardboard from around the neighborhood and the local grocery store and used it to build an office in the corner of the room, complete with walls to the ceiling. It had a door and a lock and a cardboard duct to route in air conditioning. Big Jack was happy and productive. Nick had a meeting with him in the new office and found it pleasant, with framed art on the walls and a small refrigerator in the corner filled with cans of sweet iced coffee.

Chapter Twenty-One

That Saturday, Willie and Nick beached *Caprice* on the Kaneohe Sandbar in Kaneohe Bay. The tide was out and less than a foot of water covered the sandbar, much of it only ankle deep. With turquoise water and pure white sand, it was a dazzling place. Sometimes there were weddings and big parties. That day nine other boats, including two dive boats, had pulled up on the sand. People were scattered across the sandbar, lounging, playing volleyball, and grilling food.

Willie and Nick walked around *Caprice* and inspected the catamaran, then sat in the shallow water in the boat's shade and scrubbed the hull with stiff brushes.

"How's it going with the consulting job?" Willie asked, rinsing his brush in the water.

"It's going well, I guess. Blaine uses the word 'cool' a lot, and I have concerns about the other officers."

"Why's that?"

"They don't give me the impression they are qualified to do their jobs." Nick described the officers and their backgrounds.

"They sound more like a band than a company. Do they know you play piano?"

"They don't even know I live on a boat."

They continued their task, accompanied by the music from a nearby dive boat until they heard shouts from a neighboring group. They stood up to investigate and walked to the edge of the sandbar where a crowd had gathered watching splashes and fins in the water.

"Hammerheads," Willie said.

"I heard the shark population in the bay has increased a lot in the last couple of years," Nick said.

"Sharks?" asked a woman standing next to Nick.

"Don't worry, they are after the hammerhead pups, not you," Nick told her.

"Unless you act like food," Willie added, "then they'll be after you."

Back at *Caprice*, they resumed scrubbing the hull after getting bottles of beer off the boat.

"You seem to be going through a dry spell," Willie said.

Nick stopped scrubbing and turned to face him. "What's she like?" Nick asked.

"What do you mean?"

Nick looked at Willie over his sunglasses.

"Okay, I have a woman I want you to meet," Willie said.

"She wouldn't have you?"

"No." He took a swig of beer.

"What's she like?"

"German, blonde, brilliant, petite, fit, medical student."

"Couldn't take you seriously?"

"I don't understand it," Willie said, letting out a belch. "I was even learning German."

"How did you meet?"

"Gretchen drives a Porsche. I have a Porsche. We got talking. I'm with Helena now, so it doesn't matter."

"Why do you think I should go out with her?" Nick asked.

"Someone I like should. She's fantastic. I asked her if I could give you her number. She said 'Yes'."

Nick let out a laugh. It was classic Willie. If he couldn't date a woman, he wanted one of his friends to have the opportunity. Willie had good taste in women, and the women Willie liked had discriminating taste.

"You realize the last woman I was with ran off with my friend and left me flat broke and homeless." Nick paused. "Not that I'm complaining."

It was Willie's turn to laugh. "I'm not sure I've ever heard you complain."

Chapter Twenty-Two

A nother week passed and Blaine assembled the team at a restaurant for the monthly board of directors' meeting. They had finished their meal and the server had dropped the bill at the table. Blaine took the bill and reached for his wallet.

"Ben, you're the CFO. What's twenty percent of 175?"

Ben shook his head. "I smoked way too much dope in college to figure that out."

Blaine turned to Nick.

"Thirty-five," Nick said, thinking it might be a good idea to review the company financials when he got back to the office.

Blaine continued to bring in investors. Nick spent a sizable amount of time in meetings explaining the company's product line. That day, the investors were two middle-aged men speaking in New York accents and wearing shiny dark suits. One was large and barrel-chested, the other diminutive with horn-rimmed glasses. Neither said much. Horn Rims asked a few questions of the use of the money and when the company expected to give a return. Barrel Chest sat and perspired.

While Nick presented a more directed approach with investors, Blaine's approach tended toward the informal. First, he took them to a lunch at *House Without a Key,* the restaurant at the *Halekulani Hotel* in Waikiki. They sat outside and listened to the music while the resident dancer, Kanoe, performed a hula. The dancing intrigued the men in shiny black suits. They ordered the spaghetti. Blaine had the cheeseburger with fries. Nick ordered the ahi sashimi and Manoa lettuce salad.

After lunch, Blaine treated the investors to a sail. They drove by *Icarus* at the Ala Wai Boat Harbor and boarded a sailboat Blaine borrowed from a friend for the afternoon.

With the investors on board and Blaine at the wheel, he motored out of the harbor and turned left toward Diamond Head.

The trade winds were blowing fifteen to twenty miles an hour, with gusts to thirty, not uncommon in the islands. Blaine winched in the mainsail and sailed close-hauled into the wind, an uncomfortable point of sail, pounding into the seas and heeled over.

"I'm thinking of buying this boat for the company," Blaine said to the investors, who nodded and braced themselves.

Blaine enjoyed himself, oblivious of the discomfort of his passengers, drinking his third beer of the afternoon.

The two men held on to the rail, their faces taking on a green cast. Nick moved to the helm. "Mind if I have a turn?"

"What? Yeah, okay, I guess. You know how to sail?"

"I think I can manage." Nick gently pushed Blaine away from the wheel, turned downwind, and eased the mainsheet. The ride smoothed, and the boat leveled. The men looked up at Nick with gratitude. Horn Rims got up and stood beside Nick.

"Do you have to mutiny often?" he asked.

When they got back to the dock, Nick saw he had missed a call from Sam. When he returned the call, Sam said, "Your engine arrived."

Nick heard the sounds of the boatyard in the background.

"That's great. When can we install it?"

"I already made the attachment points and fittings. I just need to break loose a couple of hours to slide it in, probably in the next day or two."

Chapter Twenty-Three

Back at the house that evening, Nick was alone. He had no idea of the whereabouts of Flibby, and Casandra was on Maui with *The Specter*. Nick was sitting on his bed, and Zeke was beside the laptop on the bedside table in his evening position. They had grown used to each other, buddies in a tropical paradise. Earlier in the evening, Nick had tried to feed him an ant or two. Zeke ignored them, looking up at Nick in his bored lizard way.

Nick wrote in his journal by the dim bedside light, catching up on documenting his ever-changing life. *I'm not in a rut, that's for sure.* He finished writing and put his journal and fountain pen on the bedside table.

"Goodnight, Zeke."

He laid back and closed his eyes and drifted off.

A couple of hours later, he tried to focus on a gossamer sight of a young woman with long, brown locks floating above him. A white gown billowed around her.

Nick wasn't afraid, just curious. When he was younger, he remembered his grandfather telling him of having such visions.

But this was a first for him. His grandfather also told Nick what to say to one.

The apparition appeared calm, friendly even. He squinted and thought he saw a smile.

"You need to continue on your way," Nick said.

The form grew brighter and then faded away.

The next morning Nick awoke at his usual time and was writing in his journal about the odd dream he had the night before when he heard a noise from under the house. He put on shorts, a t-shirt, and slippers and walked outside and through the open storm doors into the basement to find a man shuffling through stored boxes.

Nick cleared his throat.

The man turned to him. "Oh, hello. I'm Bill, the landlord," he said.

"I'm Nick."

They shook hands.

"This is my family's home. Cassandra and Persephone are the first tenants since my wife, mother, and I moved to Aina Haina. Are you a boyfriend?"

"No, I'm renting a room for a month while I'm fixing up my place."

Bill reached for a box and opened it.

"Ah, here it is!" he added, pulling a white gown from a box and holding it up. Nick felt a chill shoot through him.

"My mother passed away last night. She had wished to be buried in her wedding gown."

After Bill left, Nick sat in the covered sunporch drinking his morning coffee. Zeke skittered across the woven *lauhala* mat on the living room floor and stopped at the threshold of the front door.

"Good morning, Zeke." *It's good my roommates are gone for the weekend; I would look like a lunatic talking to a lizard.*

Zeke walked out the front door, climbed up, and perched on the chair next to Nick, letting out a chirp. The two of them looked out at Manoa Valley, like a man and his dog, but not.

"I'll be putting my boat in the water tomorrow. Then I'll say goodbye."

Zeke climbed down from the chair and made his way to the edge of the front steps. He stopped and turned back toward Nick, pausing a moment, then turned and made his way down the steps and into the yard.

Chapter Twenty-Four

It took longer than he expected, and it cost more than planned, but with the new engine installed, *Icarus* was ready to go back in the water. Nick assembled a crew for the relaunch. Willie, Helena, and Nigel were in attendance, and a small gathering of onlookers was on hand to watch and help.

It's beautiful and frightening to see an old boat cradled in slings, taken off of its blocks and lifted and moved to the water. It takes the right equipment and the right operator to do it without damaging a boat, particularly a wooden boat. But Nick had hired the right man in Sam, and he and Nick took slow, painstaking efforts to prepare *Icarus* for her trip back to the water. Sam gave the team a serious talk regarding how careful they had to be and instilled in them a sense of responsibility for the task. The entire group, stationed around the boat, took the job to heart, each holding on to a line to guide it. Sam calmly called orders to the crew to loosen one line and pull in on another as they gently lowered *Icarus* back into the water.

The crew climbed on board and Nick and Sam started the engine and let it run, watching the gauges and exhaust, listening for problems. Once Sam completed his checklist, he gave the okay for Nick to leave.

The Volvo was much quieter than the old Detroit Diesel and had more than twice the horsepower. Motoring out of Kewalo Basin, past Ala Moana Beach Park and back to the slip in the Ala Wai Boat Harbor, Nick felt the increase in power and responsiveness.

Once he and Willie thoroughly inspected the boat, they took *Icarus* offshore for a shakedown cruise. Satisfied the boat was in fine working order, Nick anchored off Waikiki for lunch and a swim.

Back at the dock, *Icarus* looked and felt like a new boat—polished and painted, the brass shining. Nick dropped below and admired the cabin. The cushions were clean, and the floor polished along with the woodwork. He had touched up the white paint in the cabin and scrubbed the prisms channeling light below the deck.

With his crew departed, Nick sat in the cockpit, overjoyed to be back in his home, to be away from the drama of roommates. A couple walked by the gate to the dock, laughing, sharing an intimacy. They held hands, smiles plastered on their faces, walking at a brisk pace—off to the beach, Nick assumed.

Loneliness fell on him like a shadow and he felt a hollowness creep into him.

That evening, Nick and Nigel made a last trip to the house in Manoa Valley.

"I came to get the rest of my things and say goodbye. Where's Flib—erm, I mean Persie?" Nick asked, meeting Cassandra at the front door as he was entering.

"Can you believe it? Persephone left," Cassandra said, spitting out her name.

"What do you mean she left? Her car is still outside."

"She's gone—moved to the mainland—flew out this morning. She sent me a text from the airport."

Nick walked across the living room to Flibby's open bedroom door. He poked his head in to see clothes strewn about the place. Piles of magazines were on the floor and the bedside table.

"It looks like she still lives here," Nick said.

"Not anymore. She didn't even tell me she was leaving."

"Jeeze, what a hole," Nigel said, standing next to Nick at the door, looking into the room.

Cassandra scoffed and left the house. They heard her start her car and leave. Nick's mobile phone rang and he answered.

"Nick, it's Persie."

"Yes, hello Persie. Cassandra told me you left this morning. Your sister is really put off."

"Yeah, Cassie told me she and Tom are talking about getting married. I had to leave before things blew up. I didn't even stop to put on a bra."

"Didn't even have time to put on a bra, eh?" Nick repeated for Nigel's benefit.

"It was nice having you for a roommate. Let me know if anyone wants to buy my car," she said.

"Okay, I will. Safe travels."

They hung up.

"She was kind of hot," Nigel said.

"We need to find you a girlfriend."

"What about you, Nick?"

The hollowness Nick felt earlier again took hold.

"Yes, we need to find me a girlfriend as well."

Chapter Twenty-Five

It was a sultry Tuesday evening and Nick had finished eating dinner an hour before Nigel showed up on his dock.

"I'm heading down to the Harbor Pub for an adult libation. Care to join me?" Nigel asked.

"Sure, let me close up." Nick turned on the air conditioner to have it cool for sleeping when he returned.

When they entered the pub, the staff and other local regulars greeted them. They found a table and ordered drinks.

"So Nigel."

"Yes, Nick?"

"I've been meaning to ask you. *Awkward Lizard*. That's quite a name for a boat, even taking into account the penchant for boat owners to go overboard on their boat names," Nick said.

Their drinks came, a whisky for Nigel and a Stella Artois beer for Nick.

"Overboard. Right." Nigel took a sip. "It came to me in a dream. I dreamt I purchased the *Awkward Lizard Vineyard* in France and then named my boat after the vineyard. I woke up and wrote the name so I wouldn't forget it. The next morning, there it was in my notebook, *Awkward Lizard*. The previous owner and his wife never agreed on a name and I hadn't come up with one yet."

"Well, that makes perfect sense."

"I even bought the dot com domain," Nigel said, taking another sip.

"Awkward Lizard dot com. I'm sure that was available."

Nigel, a commodities trader, worked his own hours and traveled often. From *Icarus,* Nick could see him working at all hours on his laptop on the stern of his boat. Nigel had been searching for a condominium in town to buy. Then he saw a flyer for a boat for sale. The boat was a tenth of the price of any condo he liked, and he made an appointment to see it. It was owned by a couple and the wife had been relocated to the mainland. Like Nigel, the husband teleworked, and it didn't matter where he was. Nigel's was the first call they'd had on the boat in months. They offered to make him an excellent deal if he was willing to move quickly on the purchase. Nigel had the boat surveyed and found it well-maintained. He figured to pay cash for it with half his down payment on the condo, and the slip fees were the same as a homeowner association payment. He would own the boat free and clear, have the same monthly outlay, less a mortgage payment, and even have money left over for a refit.

Like many people who spend time on boats in Hawaii, he had his name on a waiting list for a slip in the Ala Wai Harbor for many years. When he bought the boat, he moored it in the Ke'ehi Lagoon off of Sand Island and near the airport. He lived aboard the 51 foot coastal cruiser for two years, rowing to his boat in the evenings after working in a rented office downtown. When a slip opened up in the Ala Wai Harbor, he moved the boat there. He had to wait another year for a live-aboard permit. After completing an extensive refit, he used the boat as his home and office. He turned it into an elegant, comfortable live-aboard with the amenities of a home, including a full galley, air conditioning, and an ice maker for his American guests.

Chapter Twenty-Six

Back in his place under the dodger on *Icarus*, Nick took in the sounds of the early evening. There was a low level din like any city—a mix of traffic and people talking or yelling, and clinking of dish ware and silverware clanking at the nearby restaurants. It struck him how one could be lonely in the middle of all that humanity.

Nick took his mobile phone from his pocket and scrolled through his call list and dialed Gretchen—the German, blonde, brilliant, petite, fit medical student who couldn't take Willie seriously.

"This is Gretchen," she answered.

"Hello, my name is Nick Thomas. Willie Lee gave me your number and suggested I give you a call."

"What? Oh, Willie. Right. Hi, Nick. Please hold on a moment."

Nick took the time to take a sip of water and enjoy the view. The sky had wisps of clouds and the trade winds were light. It was the golden hour, right before sunset, and the sky took on a warm glow.

"I'm back. I needed to get off of another call. Sorry, I'm busy right now."

"I understand."

"Okay, I have to go. Bye."

"Bye," Nick said, setting his phone down.

I guess I know where I stand there.

Nearly two weeks later, Nick was again sitting on *Icarus* waiting for the sun to set when his phone rang. He picked it up and glanced at the caller ID. He looked back at the horizon and thought for a moment, let it ring a third time, then answered.

"Hello, Gretchen. How have you been?"

"Hello, Nick. I'm fine. Are you free for dinner Friday night?" she asked.

It was approaching one in the morning, and Nick was in the passenger seat of a classic Porsche Carrera traveling at 115 mph. They were on H-2 in the middle of Oahu, streaking past the towns of Mililani and Wahiawa. He had his feet braced and was holding on tight. Gretchen, at the wheel, kept her eyes on the road when she talked.

"You get the most out of your car," Nick said, tightening his grip.

"My uncle was an engineer at the Porsche factory in Zuzenhausen near Stuttgart. He taught me to drive."

Earlier that evening Gretchen met Nick in Waikiki at the Chart House, a restaurant within walking distance of *Icarus*. The Chart House and the Harbor Pub in the basement were Nick's local hangouts. He had stopped in a few days before and secured a table overlooking the harbor.

They met out front. He wore slacks and an aloha shirt printed with hibiscus and surfboards. Her short, light dress fluttered in the tropical breeze.

"You live on a boat? That's romantic," Gretchen said.

"Yes, I suppose it is."

The wine they ordered had arrived at the same time the fireworks started, launched from the beach a block away. Close, bright, and loud, they echoed off the high-rise buildings and reflected in the harbor. The vibrations from the fireworks set off car alarms.

"Is this for me?" Gretchen asked.

"I'd like to say yes, but there are fireworks every Friday night."

"It was a nice thought," she said, lifting her glass in a toast.

"*Prost!*" Gretchen said.

"*Yamas,*" Nick countered.

They watched the fireworks until they ended.

"I don't get out much and haven't heard about the fireworks. I guess I've had my head down in the books too much. Now that I see them, they are hard to miss."

Dinner came, and they ate for a while.

"I'm surprised you didn't call," Gretchen said.

"A couple of weeks ago you said you were too busy to talk. I didn't want to seem creepy."

"I was busy that day, but I have time now. How do you know I wasn't playing hard-to-get?"

Nick laughed. "In this era? There is no hard-to-get, at least not for me. If a woman doesn't show interest, I don't either."

"Sometimes a girl wants to be pursued," Gretchen whispered.

"And sometimes mixed messages can get a man into trouble."

A man and a woman arrived at the table with guitar and ukulele.

"Do you have anything you would like us to play?"

"Green Rose Hula?" Nick asked.

"Ah, excellent choice," the woman said.

"It's one of my favorites," Nick said.

The couple played the song, Nick tipped them, and they moved to the next table

"That was nice," Gretchen said.

Gretchen wanted a tour of *Icarus,* and after dinner they walked to the dock. Nick unlocked the hatch and showed her below.

Gretchen looked around. "Wow, this is really neat and clean, spotless even." She eyed Nick. "Do you always keep it in this condition?"

"I'd like to tell you I do, but no. She went back in the water a few weeks ago. I took advantage of the time to give her a thorough cleaning. It will be a lot of work to keep her this way."

Nick showed Gretchen around the boat, explaining what things were and how they worked. The gimbaled stove intrigued her.

She poked her head into the forward bunk where Nick slept. "That's cozy."

They moved back to the stern and sat under a perfect Hawaiian evening sky.

"Would you like something to drink?" Nick offered.

"Do you have any coffee?"

"Sure, I have excellent coffee."

"Coffee would be nice. I need to study later."

"Would you like anything in it?"

"If it's excellent coffee, black is fine."

Nick dropped below and turned on the kettle for the French press and ground the beans. In a while, he returned to the stern with two mugs, handed one to her, and sat down.

She took a sip. "This *is* excellent coffee. It sure is peaceful here, even surrounded by all this civilization."

"Odd, isn't it? There is something about boats in a harbor."

Gretchen took another sip. "Why do they call boats 'She'? Isn't that misogynistic?"

"Misogynistic? No, I'd say it's the opposite."

"Why do you say that?"

"The Latin word for 'ship', *Navis,* is feminine. In the past, they dedicated ships to goddesses and mother figures who protected sailors crossing vast oceans."

"So it's about boys and their mothers?"

Nick laughed. "I don't think I would take it that far, but it's as good a theory as any. It's a moot point; times are changing. Even Lloyds of London, the maritime insurer, no longer refers to ships as 'she'."

They sipped coffee and talked about life on the island. After midnight, Nick walked her back to her car. She had parked near the boat.

"This is me."

"Yes, Willie said you drove a Porsche."

"It's early and I do my best studying in the middle of the night. Care to go for a drive?"

"Sure."

"Do you usually drive this fast?" Nick asked as they sped through the island night.

"Only after dark and when the traffic is light," Gretchen replied. "You don't have to worry. I keep the in car top condition, like how you keep your boat."

"I'm not worried," Nick said. He glanced at Gretchen, appearing relaxed and focused, her eyes darting from the gauges to the road. There was no music playing on the stereo. She was in the moment, one with the car.

Nick had never felt threatened by strong, competent women. Gretchen was all that and more.

The following Sunday afternoon, Nick took *Icarus* offshore and gave Gretchen a sailing lesson. He stood behind her at the wheel to give her tips and watched her smooth and even movements. She didn't saw away at the wheel, over-correcting like many novices.

"This is the most fun I've had since I began medical school," she said. They beat upwind to Diamond Head. She had a smile plastered on her face.

She's a lot more comfortable than those guys from New York.

Once past Diamond Head, Nick instructed her in turning

the boat and sailing downwind back to Waikiki. In a strong following sea, Gretchen quickly adjusted to the different point of sail. She was a natural at the helm.

"Can we do this again next Saturday?" Gretchen asked when they returned to the dock.

Chapter Twenty-Seven

More investors flowed through the office. Nick met with them, put on a show, and introduced them to the team in the production area. Ben presented the numbers. None of the investors Blaine brought in showed any interest in the state of the company's finances, or the product development process, or the abilities of the team. They were interested in when they could take their money out of the company.

"You mean the return on investment?" Nick asked one Chicago-based investor one afternoon.

"Yeah, that's it, the return on our investment."

A knock on the conference room door interrupted them.

The FedEx delivery person came into the room with a package. "The note on the door said for me to come to the conference room."

"Hi, Julia," Nick said, reaching for the package. "Thanks."

"No problem, Nick."

When Julia left, the man from Chicago said, "You're on a first name-basis with your FedEx gal?"

"She's an important person. She brings us documents nearly every day."

"How about that?" He paused for a moment, thinking. "I'm sure we can invest in your little group here. I mean, it's all about the people, right? I heard that somewhere."

The following week, Blaine Daniels traveled to Belgium for a conference on medical software. Before he left, he dropped by Nick's office.

"I want to buy a castle for a new European division of the company," he told Nick in his conspiratorial way.

"We have a new European division?"

"My associates think it would be a good idea," Blaine said.

"Your associates? You have associates?" Nick asked.

"The investors have an interest in a castle in Belgium."

The Hawaii company had yet to earn income. The burn rate was out of control; the company bled cash. *How did Blaine expect to buy a castle and who were Blaine's associates? Why was the company going to buy a castle for the investors?*

On the way back to his office, Nick took a new bound notebook from the supply cabinet. He sat and thought for a moment and made notes, documenting the events that had happened since he joined the company. He drew a diagram of the various entities Blaine had acquired and was planning to acquire and how they related, or didn't relate, to the company. Several hours later, he had filled dozens of pages.

Heading out the door that evening, Nick walked by Blaine's office. He and Jurgis were sitting in chairs in front of the desk, talking in low tones. Blaine looked up as Nick passed by, then got up and closed the door.

Chapter Twenty-Eight

Nick and Gretchen had a natural comfort together, and Gretchen dropped by *Icarus* to study in the early evening. Her freshmen roommates, away from home for the first time, made studying at her house an unproductive experience and she grew tired of trekking to the library on campus.

Before they knew it, Nick and Gretchen had fallen into a groove. Despite her comment of "sometimes a girl wants to be pursued," Gretchen made it clear she did not want a physical relationship. Weeks passed with them spending time together on the boat, going for runs through Kapi'olani Park, and taking *Icarus* for Saturday morning sails. They often cooked and ate together or had a meal at a nearby restaurant. Nick was happy to have the companionship and resolved himself to being her friend. Between the new job and putting the finishing touches on *Icarus,* he had more than enough to keep himself occupied.

Nick and Gretchen spent most of their time together on board. She and Nick sat under the dodger in the early evenings, she studying with a fierce concentration and he doing the unending work on the boat. One afternoon Nick took a break from maintenance and sketched boats in the harbor.

"May I look?" Gretchen asked, setting down her notes.

"Sure." He handed her his sketchbook.

She flipped through it slowly. "These are nice. You have a good eye," she said.

She turned to the page with the drawing of a Polynesian woman. Gretchen studied the drawing for a while and said, "You must have really been in love with her."

Nick's face turned red. It had been a while since he had thought of Tehani in Tahiti.

"I had a huge crush on her," he admitted.

"And?"

"And, nothing. She was involved with a friend of mine and off-limits. I left town before I made an ass of myself."

He paused.

"I hope."

As Willie said, Gretchen was a German, blonde, brilliant, petite, fit medical student. He could add complicated and interesting. She was also serious and laughed little, traits Nick put down to the pressures of medical school.

Over time, he got to know her better. Her parents, after a honeymoon tour of the United States, wanted to move there permanently, and her father enlisted in the US military to obtain citizenship. However, when the Air Force learned he was fluent in both German and English, they posted him to Ramstein Air Base in Germany, a few kilometers from his family home in Bad Dürkheim, a Germany wine-growing region.

Gretchen, her sister and brother were born in the hospital at Ramstein and had dual US-German citizenship. Gretchen's sister resided in Manhattan, and her brother followed in the footsteps of their father and joined the US Air Force. They were independent children and, like their parents, of a serious nature.

For a couple of weeks after they met, Gretchen left *Icarus* for home around 10:00 p.m. so she could rise early and get to the University for her early morning classes.

One Friday afternoon three weeks after their first date, Nigel brought by a half of an *Ono* he had caught that afternoon. Nick and Nigel often shared groceries and supplies they bought, spreading the volume amongst their limited on-board storage.

That night Nick grilled the fish, and he and Gretchen had a fine meal under the dodger. After dinner, Nick cleared the plates and washed the dishes. When he came back on deck, Gretchen had her book bag open and her books spread on the table. Nick saw she was back in *Gretchen mode*, so deep in concentration she didn't notice him standing in front of her. He crawled into the forepeak cabin and opened *Fate Is the Hunter* by Earnest Gann, a book describing the author's experiences during the infancy of commercial aviation. Willie had given him the book the previous Sunday and Nick was eager to get started on it.

Hours later, he had dozed off and was vaguely aware of Gretchen covering him with a light blanket and joining him on the bunk. Nick reached over and felt a smooth, naked body beside him.

"Are you awake?" she whispered.

"I can be."

"Good," she said, crawling on top of him.

"That was unexpected," Nick said. It was an hour later and Gretchen, curled up on her side, had her head on his shoulder, hair fanned out across his chest.

She kissed him on the cheek. "This is nice," she said. "I must have been driving you crazy."

"Somewhat."

"You are very patient. Why didn't you make another move?" she asked.

"Are you kidding me? You made it abundantly clear you were off-limits."

"That was a couple weeks ago," Gretchen said, sliding her leg on top of his.

"You're easy to be around," Nick said, stroking her hair, "and you didn't give me any indication that you had changed your mind."

"Well, I have," she said, throwing the blanket off of them and crawling on top of him again.

The next morning, Nick awoke to the smell of freshly brewed coffee. As he lay in the bunk, he considered Gretchen. He hadn't planned to sleep with her until he knew where he stood. He still had no idea.

He made his way to the main cabin and saw Gretchen standing at the stove wearing nothing but one of his long sleeve linen shirts. A beam of light made its way through a deck prism and onto her golden hair. Nick took in the sight of her, watching her sure movements, the way she cocked her hip as she waited for the kettle to boil.

They spent the entire Saturday together, strolling along the sands of Waikiki toward Diamond Head, making their way to

San Souci Beach, where they had a late lunch at the *Hau Tree Lanai.*

From then on, Gretchen spent nights on the boat and their relationship took on more depth. They talked for hours when she wasn't studying. She was the first woman he had seriously dated since his wife ran off with Lance.

Gretchen had no other friends, and she didn't interact with her classmates. Nick was one of the few people she spent time with. She preferred to stay behind to study rather than join the crew on the Sunday sails on Willie's catamaran.

One Friday evening on *Icarus,* Nick and Gretchen were having a glass of wine after the fireworks when Nick said, "You haven't met many people in Hawaii."

"No, I haven't. My roommates are a couple of idiots and I don't think much of my classmates." She paused. "In fact, I find most people to be frivolous and uninteresting."

"You're a classic misanthrope."

Gretchen took a sip of wine, put the glass down, and leaned back into a cushion. "I suppose you're right. But I like you."

"Well, thank you. I like you, too. But, if you don't like most people, why do you want to be a doctor?"

Gretchen thought about it for a moment.

"I like to fix things."

Chapter Twenty-Nine

When Nick arrived for work the next morning, he saw Blaine's office door ajar. He poked his head in. The office was empty, and on the edge of Blaine's desk was a pile of papers. The one on the top caught Nick's eye—a transfer receipt from the *National Commercial Bank, Jamaica Ltd of the Cayman Islands.* Some of the investment dollars came from offshore accounts. He took a picture of the document with his phone, left the building, walked down the street to the local coffee shop, and ordered an espresso.

Nick thought about how little control people have over events that happen in life. He knew it's how one responds to those events wherein the power lies.

He sat sipping his coffee and pondered his options.

Nick was familiar with the *National Commercial Bank, Jamaica Ltd. of the Cayman Islands,* the first stop for his money when Lance, his business partner, stole it. From there, Lance scattered the money to the wind, moving it around the globe in a series of electronic transfers, making it untraceable.

Nick shuddered, recalling the hell Lance had put him through.

"Not again," he said out loud to himself.

Not everyone uses offshore banks for nefarious means. But he would need to pay careful attention from now on, if only to keep himself out of trouble.

He finished his coffee and headed back to his office.

Chapter Thirty

The next day, during a meeting with another mainland investment group, Nick sat in on a presentation by Ben, the CFO. It was a typical talk about how the money would be used and what return on investment could be expected. It was *boilerplate*, the same items as in any financial presentation. There was one glaring difference, however.

The numbers were wrong.

In Ben's presentation, the company showed revenue. The company had yet to make a penny, but the balance sheet showed more than $6 million in revenue. Nick sat at the table and studied the spreadsheet in front of him. Maybe he read the wrong column. No, he was seeing it correctly.

Nick had to ask. "Ben, the revenue in row 24 comes from what source?"

The heads at the table looked down at their papers. Ben scanned down with his finger.

"Row 24. Oh, that came from the investors."

Nick turned to him. "You mean stock sales?"

"Right. Stock sales," Ben said.

Nick looked up at Blaine and Claire and the investors.

Blaine glared at him. The others were bored and unconcerned with the outright incompetence and possible fraud. Maybe they didn't know the difference or care the CFO reported stock investment as income. In generous terms, it was a mistake. In the harshest of terms, it was a Ponzi scheme—making investors think revenue is coming from legitimate business activity, when in fact, other investors are the source of the funds.

Nick felt the need to make it clear to the men across the table. "You understand these numbers are incorrect and this company has shown no income? We wouldn't want you to think any different."

"Yeah, we get it; there's no income," the leader of the investors said. "But we still want to invest."

Later in the week, when the vote came up to buy the castle in Belgium, Nick was the only dissenting vote among the board of directors. He slid the profit-and-loss statement across the table to Ben and leaned forward.

"Ben, how can you vote to buy a castle when we won't be able to make payroll this month?"

Ben picked up the paper, examined it, and turned to Blaine. Blaine stared blankly back at Ben. Ben shrugged.

Blaine sat silently, looking at Claire and Ben, avoiding looking at Nick.

"We'll have more investment money in time to pay the employees."

Ben turned to Nick. "See? We'll have the money."

Nick turned to Blaine, who still avoided eye contact with him. He sat back in his chair.

"Good to know," he said.

Chapter Thirty-One

Blaine Daniels grew up in the small mining town of Globe, Arizona, a place well documented in history books with gun fights, stagecoach robberies, and raids by the local Apache tribe. It was also the home of Mary Kate Horony, known as *Big Nose Kate*, the paramour of gun fighter Doc Holliday, famous for his involvement in the gunfight at the O.K. Corral.

The mines in Globe first produced silver, and when silver played out, copper. Turquoise, a by-product of copper mining, gets its blue color from the copper element. The Sleeping Beauty Mine in Globe produced what jewelers consider to be the finest turquoise ever to come out of the ground. When the mine closed in 2012, the Chinese, who prized the clean, rare turquoise, bought up the rest. There are copper and uranium mines, gas and oil wells, and rock quarries still active in Globe. Since the early 1900s, the population count had changed little, bouncing between 6000 and 7500 people. The largest employer is the prison in Florence, 50 miles away, where Blaine Daniels' father was serving time for larceny. A charismatic man, he had the markings of a successful career in grifting. Narcissistic, lacking empathy, and with a true Machiavellian streak, he sold shares in mines scattered throughout Arizona. He found remote, defunct, abandoned mines in the desert and forged mines shares for existing mines and sold shares in mines that did not exist. Blaine Daniels' father staged the mine to make it look active, even going to the trouble to salt the mine with whatever precious commodity was going to get attention. Silver and copper were his favorites. For one scheme, he rented a tractor, drove into the desert, dug a hole in the side of a hill, planted some turquoise, and sold the entire mine to an easily excitable investor. If it weren't for a visiting out-of-town sheriff looking to hit it rich, Blaine Daniels' father would probably still be on the outside of the prison walls rather than within them. The mines, the prison, and other factors made Globe one of the most dangerous towns in Arizona.

While their father served time, Blaine Daniels' mother worked long, hard hours as a nurse at the local hospital to keep a roof over their heads', and food on the table for her two young boys.

There wasn't much to do in Globe for a chubby boy like Blaine Daniels. His brother was athletic and fit. Blaine Daniels was neither.

Young Blaine spent most of his time alone. He bought a BB gun at a local trading post, got on his bicycle, rode the old mine trails, and shot at anything presenting itself as a target. Along the way, he amassed a collection of rocks and minerals. Near the mines he found specimens of Sleeping Beauty Turquoise, brilliant green malachite, intense blue azurite, and chunks of copper.

In the summer months when the mercury rose, Blaine Daniels sat in his bedroom and watched movies while an old rusted air conditioner rattled in the window. One day, at a thrift store in town, he came across boxes of *film noir* movies. They had been collecting dust in the back of the shop for years. When the owner of the shop saw Blaine Daniels looking at the tapes, he offered him the lot for five dollars. He even threw in an old VCR to play them.

The first film he watched was *Double Indemnity*, about a woman who wanted her insurance salesman husband dead and would collect double the insurance payout if the death were deemed an accident. Next he watched the *Maltese Falcon, The Third Man, The Big Sleep*, and from the 1970s, *Chinatown*.

But unlike the hard-nosed detectives Philip Marlowe, Sam Spade, and the brutal Mike Hammer depicted in those movies, he related more to their antagonists. Blaine Daniels took after his father.

He always wanted to be a bad guy.

Chapter Thirty-Two

A father and daughter prepared dinner on their sailboat *Raison d'erte* moored in the Ke'ehi Lagoon near the airport. They had left New Zealand a month before and when they arrived in Hawaii, they went into town to provision the boat for the next leg of their journey. They were most eager to buy fresh fruits and vegetables as they had been living off of their stores and the fish they caught.

Later, back at the boat, while the sunset took on color, they barbecued steak and chicken and an assortment of fresh vegetables. Hawaiian music played on the cockpit stereo. They always listened to the local music of whatever port they were in.

"It's the wrong time of year to be sailing from here to California," the father said, turning food on the grill. "We are going to have a very slow passage or motor most of our way across the Pacific. What do you say we tour the islands for a month or so? Start with Moloka'i and head on to Maui?"

"I don't start graduate school until January. That gives us plenty of time to get to the West Coast." She took a bottle from the ice bucket on the floor of the cockpit and poured two glasses of wine. She handed one to her father.

"I am very proud of you, Adriana. You find what is interesting to you and you dive in all the way." He lifted his glass in a toast.

"Thank you, Daddy. You have always been supportive of my whims."

They both took sips of wine.

"Can we head to the outer islands tomorrow? Honolulu has turned into a big city. I will get enough of that in California," Adriana asked.

"I was thinking the same thing," said her father.

Chapter Thirty-Three

After the last investor meeting, Nick felt it was time to consult the company's attorney regarding the legal ramifications of the CFO's behavior to learn if the company was breaking any laws. The office was empty except for Ben, who had his head down and was moaning into his computer screen.

Darby Jurgis sauntered in a half an hour late for his meeting with Nick. He wore his ill-fitting gray three-piece suit. He reminded Nick of a homeless guy in San Francisco he had once given $100 to when he had little himself.

Nick led Jurgis to the conference room.

"What can I do for you?" Jurgis asked.

Nick open his notebook and read his concerns. They included Ben, the CFO reporting investment as income and Blaine buying foreign real estate with investment dollars while the company couldn't make payroll.

Nick paused between each point, giving Jurgis an opportunity to comment. Jurgis sat placidly. The yellow legal pad and a stubby, worn-down pencil in front of him remained idle. Nick finished and waited for Jurgis to comment.

"Those are interesting concerns you have. I'll give them some thought," Jurgis said after a lingering silence.

Nick sat dumbfounded as Jurgis gathered his still-blank pad and pencil and turned and left the room.

That afternoon, on the way to *Icarus,* Nick stopped off at the post office to collect his mail. When he got on board, the air conditioner was on and Gretchen was studying in the saloon. She leaned forward for a kiss without taking her eyes off her work.

Nick changed into shorts and a T-shirt in the forepeak cabin, took a bottle of water from the cooler, and headed to the cockpit. Gretchen, so engrossed in her studies, didn't look up when he passed. He sat under the dodger and took a sip of water. He figured Blaine and Darby had looked him up online and found the news articles about the investigation of him for embezzlement. Maybe they believed Nick was 'one of them' and he had gotten away with it. There were people who always believe the worst, that Nick stole his own money. One of the bright sides of Nick losing everything and being a suspect in his own demise was he no longer felt the need to seek approval, or worry about what other people thought of him. In fact, he worried little since he started his life over.

Chapter Thirty-Four

That Friday, as Nick walked past Blaine's office, he saw an object on the white carpet just inside the door. He reached down and picked it up. It was a faceted gemstone, the color a brilliant green.

What was a loose gemstone doing on the floor of Blaine's office? He looked around. The place was already deserted. He pocketed the stone with the thought he could return it later.

The following Monday, Nick met Willie at a Thai restaurant in Kaimuki down the hill from Nick's office. Nick called ahead and reserved the private dining room, glassed-in and overlooking the rest of the restaurant. The board had eaten there occasionally and had used the room before.

The owner greeted him at the door and showed him to the room. "You said two? Not your usual group?" she said, placing two menus on the table.

"Only two, Malee." He saw Willie coming through the front door. "There he is now."

"I'll send him back."

Willie joined Nick at the table and Malee came by a few minutes later to take their lunch order.

When she left Willie asked, "How's Gretchen?"

"It was weird at first, but we are doing fine now. She has all but moved on board *Icarus*. She studies constantly and doesn't interact with many people," Nick said.

"I can't say you are rebounding from your ex-wife. It has been more than a year."

"No, I don't think I'm rebounding," Nick said. "But we seemed to have bypassed romance, and gone directly to being a couple," Nick said.

"Uh, oh."

"What do you mean, 'uh, oh'?"

"You're a romantic guy. I saw you when you were with Jody. You always put in the extra effort," Willie said.

Nick considered it. The hollowness he felt had dissipated, but it was unlike any relationship he had been in. He shrugged. "I suppose I do put in the extra effort, but not this time. It sort of just happened."

They changed the subject and were deep into a discussion of the provisions needed for their trip to Moloka'i and on to Maui, when Malee came by to fill their water glasses. As she turned to leave, Willie complained, "Why is our food taking so long?"

Malee glared at Willie over her shoulder on the way out of the room.

"Good food takes time. Are you in a hurry?" Nick asked.

"No, just hungry."

"She sure gave you stink-eye," Nick said.

Ten minutes later, the food came and they both attacked it. Nick saw beads of perspiration appearing on Willie's forehead.

"Food too spicy for you, Willie?"

"I must have really offended her," he said, wiping his brow, his paper napkin soaking through. "How's yours?"

"Perfect."

A few minutes later, Malee came by to refill their water glasses. She looked from Nick to Willie. "How come the *haole* uses chopsticks and the local boy uses a fork?"

"I like chopsticks," Nick answered.

"I don't," said Willie.

"How is the food today?" she asked.

"Excellent as always, Malee. Thank you," Nick said.

She turned to Willie. "How about yours?"

"It's wonderful. Thank you." The perspiration flowed down his forehead, down his cheeks and onto his chin.

The waitress shrugged and left the room.

"Aren't going to let her get the better of you, eh, Willie?"

"You've got that right."

"Do you know someone I can talk to about gemstones?" Nick asked between bites.

"That's an interesting request. Are things getting serious with Gretchen? You didn't mention that. You're moving a bit fast, aren't you?"

"No, it's not that."

"All right. Sure, I know a guy you can talk to."

"I need him to be discreet," Nick added.

Willie put down his fork and looked across the table at Nick. "In that case, I know another guy. What's going on, Nick?"

"Maybe something. Maybe nothing. That's what I need to find out."

Willie sat back in his chair. "Right. So there's a guy in Chinatown."

Nick took a sip of water. "Of course there is. Everything happens in Chinatown."

Having spent many of his formative years in Chinatown, Willie had a wide range of friends and acquaintances there.

On Hotel Street in Chinatown, his uncle had run the mahjong parlor that received regular raids by the Honolulu Police Department. Next door, Willie's grandmother had been the madam at one of the many Chinatown bordellos called "boogie houses." The family had made a fortune during World War II, providing services to enlisted men and officers alike. Meals at the Lee household included a cross section of the islands—politicians, kahunas, and a host of multiracial cousins, aunties, and uncles in every type of profession, lawful and not. Willie had entrée into nearly anyone in any part of the island culture.

"Do you want me to go with you and make an introduction?" Willie asked.

"No. You'd better not."

"He tends to lecture—no—more like teach, when he talks. I think of him as a professor. You'll like him. He's your type of person. I'll let him know you're coming."

After lunch, Nick made his way to Chinatown. He found the shop on Maunakea Street.

The tall Chinese man behind the counter greeted him as he came in the door.

"Are you the friend of William Lee?" he asked.

"Yes, I am. My name is Nick Thomas."

The man walked around the counter, locked the door to the shop, and turned the dial on the "Will Return" sign in the window to 1:30.

"Now we won't be disturbed. My name is Herbert Jin." They shook hands. "Let us go in the back."

Nick followed him to the back of the shop, past display cases of jade bracelets, pearl necklaces, and gold cuffs with Hawaiian writing in black. In the back room there was a large safe and a jewelry bench and a table with an array of scientific equipment.

The man gestured to a chair. Nick sat.

"Now, what can I do for you?"

"I have a gemstone and I would like to know what it is." Nick reached into his pocket. He handed an Altoids tin to Mr. Jin, who took it to his jewelry bench and turned on a lamp. He then carefully opened the tin and unwrapped the tissue containing the stone.

He reached for tweezers, picked up the stone, wiped it with a cloth, and held it up to the light. Using a loupe, he examined the stone from different angles.

"It looks like an emerald," he said. "But let's make sure."

Mr. Jin moved to his right and sat in front of a microscope. He held the stone under the lens. As he examined it, he spoke, "An emerald is made of the mineral beryl. The color comes from trace elements of chromium and sometimes vanadium. Aquamarine is also a beryl, but other trace elements color it blue. Other beryls are morganite, which is pink, and heliodor, which is yellow."

He took the gemstone from under the microscope and set it on a polishing cloth, then pulled a device off of a shelf.

"This is a refractometer, one of the most important tools for identifying gemstones." He took a light from the bench, slid it into a slot in the back of the refractometer and turned it on, then opened the cover on the top, exposing a glass plate. Taking a dark bottle off the shelf, he unscrewed the cap, and using the attached dropper, put a drop of yellow liquid on the glass plate.

"This is RI—that is—refractive index fluid. We are going to measure the refractive index of the stone. When light travels from the air into a gemstone, it changes direction."

I understand why Willie thinks of this guy as a professor.

He took the tweezers and placed the stone on the glass plate of the refractometer, then rotated the stone while looking into a lens at the front of the instrument.

"Take a look," Mr. Jin said, standing back.

Nick got up and peered into the eyepiece.

"You're looking for a green line on the scale."

"Yes, I see the line."

"Depending on the rotation of the stone, an emerald will measure between 1.565 and 1.599 on the scale. This one measures between 1.571 and 1.577." Mr. Jin made a note of the numbers on a pad of paper. "I apologize for the lecture in gemology. I find if I share my knowledge, it helps me remember the fine points of the craft."

"No apology needed," Nick said. "It's fascinating and I'm always up for learning new things."

Mr. Jin nodded. "Now we will do one more test." He took an elaborate scale from the shelf. "I will weigh the stone in air and then weigh the stone suspended in water. A simple calculation will then give us the specific gravity of the stone."

He weighed the stone and added more numbers to the pad of paper as he did, using a calculator to come up with a number. From the shelf he took a book and thumbed through it, running his finger down a column of numbers. He stopped and sat back.

"It's definitely an emerald, and of high quality." He took another book off the shelf and located another page. "Based on the clarity and color, refractive index, and specific gravity, you can get a good idea where a stone is from. Emeralds were a favorite of the ancient Egyptians, and especially Cleopatra. But, the best emeralds are usually from Columbia. But they are also mined in Brazil, Zambia, Zimbabwe, and Afghanistan. They are even found in North Carolina."

"Any idea where this one is from?" Nick asked.

Mr. Jin sat back and turned to Nick. "The color is blue green, and the clarity of the stone is excellent. The refractive index and specific gravity indicate it is from the Chivor area of Columbia, and the darkness of the stone suggests a deep mine."

"Are you looking to sell it? I may have a buyer," Mr. Jin asked.

"No, I don't think so. I wanted to know what it is."

"It is an emerald, and a fine one." Mr. Jin took the stone and cleaned it with a cloth. He then took a square of ivory colored paper, placed the emerald on it and folded the paper around the stone. He then slid the paper into a small ziplock bag, put it back in the tin, and handed it to Nick.

"Thank you. May I pay you for your time?"

"That won't be necessary. I enjoy looking at something new. It's been a while since I used this equipment. It's been getting dusty."

Mr. Jin stood up. "You are a good listener. Please give my regards to William."

"I will. Thank you."

Chapter Thirty-Five

That afternoon Nick stopped off at *Icarus* and turned on the air conditioner, made himself a cup of tea, and sat at the saloon table.

An offshore bank account, a castle in Europe, putting investment in the income column of the profit-and-loss statement, suspicious investors who don't care about their return on investment, a Giacometti statue, *and a high-quality emerald lying on the carpet in Blaine's office.*

It was too much to ignore.

Nick didn't want to be caught up in something illegal and become guilty by association. Drinking his tea, he considered his options. He picked up his phone and made a few calls, closed up *Icarus,* and drove to the office. Stopping by Blaine's office, he knocked on the door. Blaine turned from his computer.

"I'm getting nowhere with the acquisition of new computers, so I booked a flight to the mainland to break them loose." Nick asked.

"The mainland? When are you going?" Blaine sounded excited to have him leave.

"Tomorrow morning. I figure I might as well get on it right away. Not having the new equipment is slowing us down."

"That's a great idea. Have a good trip. Take all the time you need," Blaine said, turning back to his computer.

Back on *Icarus* that evening, Nick had finished packing when Gretchen called from the dock gate. He let her in, and she climbed down the companionway and into the saloon. She saw Nick's carry-on bag and leather daypack on the settee.

"Going somewhere?" she asked.

"I need to take a quick trip to the mainland."

She gave Nick a forlorn look. "Oh," she said.

He handed her a set of keys. "Would you like to stay on *Icarus* and watch over her while I'm gone?"

Her eyes lit up. "Oh, yes. That would be great. I'll take good care of her."

"I'm sure you will."

Chapter Thirty-Six

"When are you going?" Willie asked.

"Tomorrow morning, early," Nick said.

"Man, that sounds good. I need to get off this rock. Maybe I'll come with you and stay with my family in San Francisco."

The next morning when Nick arrived at the airport, the agent issued him a new boarding pass.

"This is for a first-class seat," he told the agent.

"That's right," the agent said.

Nick walked down the jetway and a flight attendant greeted him at the door of the aircraft, relieved him of his carry-on, and handed him a glass of champagne.

"This way, Mr. Thomas."

Willie sat in the second row, sipping a mai tai.

"I ordered you champagne. It's not Bollinger, but it will have to do."

"Champagne? The sun is barely over the yardarm," Nick

said, sitting down and sliding his leather backpack under the seat in front of him.

"I haven't seen you up this early since university days," Nick said.

"I didn't have a choice. You booked the early flight. The mai tai helps."

"I don't think my company is going to spring for a first-class ticket, Willie. Although, they might. They don't seem to care about money."

Willie turned to Nick. "I called a cousin at the airline. Neither of us is paying for a first class ticket."

"Well, thanks. How long are you going to be in the city?" Nick asked.

"I'll see how it goes. I bought a one-way ticket," Willie said.

They settled in for the flight and reminisced about their time together at the university and how much Hawaii had changed over the years.

Later, when they were on final approach for landing, their discussion was interrupted by a cabin announcement.

"Ladies and gentlemen, we have a little light on in the cockpit telling us the nose gear is not down and locked in place. So we're going to fly down the runway and have the tower take a look for us."

"Well, that's interesting," Nick said.

He and Willie looked out the window to the San Francisco Bay and watched as they flew over the runways and turned and climbed to the East. Other inbound aircraft were turning away from the airport.

The pilot made another announcement. "The tower couldn't

tell us much more than our nose gear is indeed down. So we're going to go ahead and land. We're going to hold the nose up until we bleed off speed, and then we'll lower the nose and see if the gear is locked. We practice this in the simulator all the time. We should be fine. Flight attendants, please prepare the cabin."

The flight attendants came on the intercom and instructed the passengers to stow their belongings and showed them how to brace themselves for landing.

"Put your wallet and phone in your pocket in case we have to leave everything when we deplane," Nick said, reaching for his day pack.

"Good idea," Willie said.

The woman across the aisle stopped the flight attendant to ask her, "Do planes crash often?"

"Only once," the flight attendant replied, moving down the aisle.

From the back of the plane, a choir began to sing *Nearer, My God, to Thee.*

"Have we died already?" Willie asked.

"I believe that's the Samoan church group that was behind me when I boarded," Nick said.

A calm came over the cabin while they waited to land, perhaps helped by the choir singing in perfect harmony.

At least it was calm until a loud bang came from the starboard side of the aircraft, followed by a jolt and bounce.

"Ladies and gentlemen, this is your captain again. It seems we will make this landing with one engine. But not to worry, we practice this too. We are going to be a little busy up here in the cockpit. We'll chat again when we get on the ground."

"If we survive this, it's going to make a great story," Willie said.

The choir increased in volume and intensity, filling the cabin and drowning out the remaining engine.

"Uh, oh." Willie gestured to the flight attendants sitting in the jump seats outside the cockpit door. They stared straight ahead, holding hands, knuckles white.

"First class is nice, but always the first at the scene of an accident," Nick said.

"First crash?"

Nick turn to Willie.

"Too soon?"

A flight attendant took the handset from its cradle and in a deadpan voice said, "Please remain in the braced position until the aircraft has come to a complete stop."

"I'm glad I only bought a one-way ticket," Willie said.

The choir reached a crescendo as the rear wheels touched down and the plane sped down the runway.

Willie and Nick watched the fire brigade catching up with the slowing airplane. The plane traveled most of the way down the runway before coming to a halt. Applause erupted throughout the aircraft.

"I think that landing will make the news," Nick said.

Willie, still looking out the window, let out a yawn.

"I'm hungry," he said.

Chapter Thirty-Seven

That afternoon, Nick sat in Jim's living room in the Santa Cruz Mountains, south of San Francisco. Jim and Nick had met in Houston while they worked in the aerospace industry. Jim Fujiyama, a retired NASA astronaut, consultant, and widower, was one of Nick's closest friends.

"I understand you had an eventful arrival," Jim said.

"You know what they say—any landing you can walk away from is a good one."

"Now that you've arrived without crashing, how long will you be here?"

"A few days. I'm meeting with a supplier in the Valley." Nick paused. "I also have a meeting scheduled with John Mitchell."

When Nick's partner, Lance Grabowski, embezzled from Nick's company and emptied his bank accounts, the San Francisco office of the FBI thoroughly investigated Nick.

John Mitchell, Special Agent in Charge, and Nick Thomas had a strange relationship of distrust and mutual respect. Mitchell found no motive for Nick to embezzle from his own company, nor could he find any evidence. The investigation pointed to Lance and Nick's ex-wife, Jody, who disappeared shortly after filing for divorce.

"You're meeting with Mitchell? FBI Mitchell? The guy who made your life hell investigating you after your friend and business partner made off with everything you had? That Mitchell?" Jim was the most loyal of friends. When Mitchell had interviewed Jim during the investigation, Jim told Mitchell, "It would be a colossal waste of time and resources pursuing Nick Thomas as a suspect in his own embezzlement."

"He was only doing his job," Nick said, taking a sip of coffee.

In the morning, Nick drove his rental car to Palo Alto to meet with the sales representative for the company computers. He thought it inane he had to make a plane trip to get a company to make a sale. He accomplished in a half an hour what he had been trying to do for a month on the phone from Hawaii.

With business completed, his next appointment was with John Mitchell, who agreed to meet him for coffee in the city of Burlingame, south of the San Francisco airport.

Nick got to the coffee shop early and ordered. They had spent so much time together during the investigation Nick knew how Mitchell liked his coffee—cream, with two sugars—and that he would show up exactly on time.

Mitchell walked through the door at 11:00 a.m.. Nick had paid for the two coffees and turned and handed Mitchell his.

"I was surprised to hear from you," Mitchell said, taking a sip. "It's perfect, thanks."

Nick motioned him to a table at the back of the coffee shop.

They sat and sipped their coffee, quiet for the moment.

"Katherine and I are no longer together," Mitchell said.

"I heard."

Nick had made plans to visit with Katherine directly after his meeting with Mitchell. He didn't see the point in mentioning it.

Katherine was Lance's ex-wife and Nick's ex-girlfriend from college. She later dated Mitchell, the man who investigated Nick.

Nick and Katherine had been exchanging emails, and she had told Nick she and Mitchell had parted company and she had begun seeing someone from their old social circle.

"I assume you didn't want to meet to buy me a cup of coffee."

"No, I'm working for a new company. I would like your take on things that are going on there."

"Okay," Mitchell said.

Nick launched into the company in Honolulu—about the strange east coast investors in the shiny dark suits with no interest in the investment, but more interested in when they would get their money back. How the CFO was categorizing stock sales as revenue and the investors knew, and Nick was the only one who cared. How the other directors had no experience or idea of how to do their jobs. How the CEO was planning a trip to Belgium to buy a castle.

Nick purged it in one long sentence. He ended with "It's like no business I've ever seen."

Mitchell sat for a moment before commenting. "It sounds like a Ponzi scheme. It's a good thing you got in touch with me."

Nick pulled his mobile phone from his pocket. He flipped through his photographs. Finding the one he wanted, he slid the phone to Mitchell. "That's a photo of a wire transfer receipt the company received from one of our investors. It was sitting on the desk of the CEO."

Mitchell picked up the phone.

"Zoom in," Nick said.

Mitchell spread his fingers across the glass. The screen filled with *National Commercial Bank, Jamaica Ltd of the Cayman Islands.*

Mitchell's eyes narrowed. "Money laundering? Where have I seen that bank before?"

"It's the same bank Lance Grabowski used when he cleaned me out," Nick said.

"Money laundering and a Ponzi scheme? You sure find the best people to work with."

Nick ignored the comment, although it hit home.

"How would they use a start-up company in Hawaii to launder money?" Nick asked.

Mitchell looked down at his empty cup. "I'll give it some thought."

Nick stood and picked up their cups. "I'll get us more coffee while you ponder it."

When Nick returned, Mitchell took a sip and launched into a lecture.

"Money laundering usually involves three phases. The first step is *placement*. Whenever an organization needs to launder their money, they move the dirty money into legitimate financial institutions, in the form of cash bank deposits. The banks and the IRS watch for deposits over ten thousand dollars. Any amount more than that and a *Suspicious Activity Report* filing is made to alert authorities of possible criminal intent, so the organization may have many people making deposits to many institutions with amounts under that threshold."

"Ten thousand dollars at a time is not much when you are dealing with big money," Nick said. "That's a lot of deposits—more than a hundred deposits for every million dollars."

"Yes. Money laundering is a business of its own. Anyway, the next phase is called *layering*. That's where the trail of money is obscured. It may involve moving money between banks, to different countries and different currencies. Usually the accounts are in different names and the amounts are different, to further obscure the money."

Mitchell stopped and drank his coffee. Nick could see he was enjoying himself.

"The layering phase may include the purchase of high-ticket items such as houses, art, boats, cars, other real estate. Diamonds are a favorite. That changes the form of the money."

"How about emeralds?" Nick asked.

"Sure, emeralds fit in that category."

Nick reached into his pocket and retrieved the gemstone and slid it across the table to Mitchell.

"I found this on the floor of the CEO's office."

Mitchell picked it up and examined it. Held it up to the light.

"Based on its color and clarity, it's probably from a deep mine in Columbia. It's high quality," Nick added.

"And you know this how?"

"I had someone examine it."

"You had it examined?"

"Discreetly."

"And you found it on the floor of Blaine Daniels', is it? Blaine Daniels' office?"

"Yes, on the floor, right inside his office door. I spotted it when I was leaving for the day."

"Did anyone see you take it?"

"No, most of the board works bankers' hours. I was alone."

Mitchell sat back in his chair and took a sip of coffee.

"I need to hold on to this," Mitchell said.

"I figured as much."

"There is also what looks like a Giacometti in the lobby," Nick said.

"Giacometti, the Italian sculptor?"

"Actually, he was Swiss and lived in Paris," Nick said.

"Really."

Nick shrugged. "I spent a lot of time in the *Musée d'Orsay* and the *Louvre* when I went to school in Paris."

Mitchell pulled a notebook and pen from his breast pocket. "Let's go over the details again."

"I've been making notes," Nick said, pulling the bound notebook from his daypack. He opened to the page of the diagram he drew of the different companies.

John Mitchell took a picture of the pages with his phone. "You always were organized," he said. "This will help a lot."

After Nick had repeated his story and spelled the names to Mitchell, they sat quietly, each in their own thoughts.

"Money laundering is a lot of work," Nick said.

"It is, but it's about making it difficult to trace the original dirty money."

"It would explain the CEO talking about buying a yacht and a castle in Belgium," Nick said.

"Perhaps. The final phase of money laundering is called *integration*. That's when the money goes back into the legitimate economy. It looks like a lawful transaction with a normal bank transfer."

A man with a laptop dropped into the seat beside Nick. Mitchell stopped talking, took another sip of coffee.

"It's a beautiful day. How would you like to sit outside on the patio? A table opened up," Nick said, gesturing to the interloper and standing up. Mitchell, having the same thought, got up and followed Nick. They sat down at a table against the wall next to a noisy fountain.

"This ought to do it," Mitchell said. "There are lots of ways Daniels could integrate the money. One is by investing in a business, such as the company in Hawaii, or buying a yacht with dollars from the layering phase and selling it in the integration phase, the same as with real estate. Sometimes a large deposit is placed and then later the purchase is canceled with maybe a penalty. The balance is refunded in clean dollars. I think buying a castle fits into that category. Other people in on the deal usually get a piece of the pie. Once the money is in the integration phase, it's difficult to prove if no documentation exists from the earlier phases."

Mitchell sat back and picked up his coffee. It had grown cold during his oratory.

"That's the traditional way of laundering money. The new wave is cryptocurrency. Some of these organizations are actually using their own version of Bitcoin. There are over 13,000 cryptocurrencies out there, and more every day. I'm surprised they're not into that," Mitchell said.

Nick took it in. "So it's probably not a Ponzi scheme. It's just a money laundering operation. The company won't make money. Not the way Blaine is running it. The investment is going to salaries, and I don't understand how they will make payroll this month."

"If they buy castles and yachts, the payroll may be a loss they are willing to accept. What are the other directors like?" Mitchell asked.

"I told you the CFO put investment dollars in the revenue column. I think he did it out of ineptitude rather than on purpose. He was a cab driver and a musician before Blaine made him CFO. Was far as I know, he has no financial background. The other director is a yoga teacher. The company attorney works out of his apartment."

Mitchell shook his head. "Their mistake is having an incompetent CFO who isn't clever enough not to call attention to the company. The other mistake was hiring someone like you who knew and cared about the difference."

"What do you suggest I do?"

"Go back to work and keep your eyes open. Let me know if you see or hear anything else suspicious. Where are you staying and how long will you be here?"

"I'm staying with Jim Fujiyama. I leave tomorrow, Friday morning, on the Hawaiian Airlines flight," Nick said.

"Jim Fujiyama, your astronaut friend?"

"Yes, that's him."

"He really laid into me when I was investigating you," Mitchell said.

"Yes, he told me. He's a great friend."

Nick reached into the breast pocket of his jacket and pulled out an envelope. "Here's a list of the investors to date and the amounts they put into the company."

Mitchell looked at his phone. "It's getting late. I'd like to get back to the office and start building a file on your company."

Nick checked his watch. "It would be good to get moving before traffic hits."

They both stood up and walked out the front door and past the covered columned entrance to the sidewalk in front of the coffee shop.

Mitchell stopped next to a mailbox, resting his arm on the top.

"What's next?", Nick asked.

"Leave your phone on. I'll be in touch."

Nick saw movement out of the corner of his eye and reached for Mitchell, grabbed his jacket and roughly pulled him away from the mailbox and both of them into the portico, slamming them against the front door of the shop.

"Hey, what gives?" Mitchell protested. He looked past Nick as a late model Chevy Nova barreled down the sidewalk, tearing the mailbox off of its legs and launching it into the air, sideswiping a row of cars as it went. It continued until it got to the next street, then swerved to the right and kept going. They could hear it continuing on its journey, the fading sound punctuated by more crashing.

Mitchell was already on his phone, calling in the incident and giving a description of the vehicle and its license plate.

He ended the call and exhaled loudly.

People from the coffee shop came out to investigate. A man walked up to Mitchell. "I saw the whole thing. You would be dead if your friend hadn't pulled you out of the way."

He turned to Nick. "That was quick thinking."

"How'd it go with the FBI?" Jim asked.

Later that afternoon, Nick was back at Jim's home, standing at the outdoor grill, cooking salmon, and drinking wine.

"It was an education. I got a crash course in money laundering," Nick said, taking the salmon off the grill.

"He thought it's worth pursuing? He is interested?" Jim asked.

"He was interested—very interested by the time he had finished his coffee."

"Money laundering, huh? At least you've covered your backside. You told the FBI you suspect there's something going on and you're not part of it."

"That's was my plan."

"Now what?" Jim asked.

It was a typical response from Jim. Nick had dealt with the problem, and it was time to move on.

"Tomorrow I'm going to go visit Katherine for coffee and Willie for lunch in the city and then head back to the islands Friday morning."

Chapter Thirty-Eight

That evening in Chinatown in Honolulu, Blaine and Jurgis sat at the Little Village Noodle House having dinner.

"More taro duck?" Jurgis asked as platters of food arrived.

"I love this stuff," Blaine said.

"I guess you do."

They ate for a while, and then Jurgis set down his chopsticks and pushed his plate away. "Nick Thomas came to see me last week."

"That guy is getting on my nerves. What did he want?"

"He had several questions."

"Such as?"

"He seemed most concerned about Ben putting income in the investment column of the profit-and-loss statement."

"I can see how that would look bad," Blaine said.

Jurgis took a sip of tea. "It makes it look like we're running a Ponzi scheme."

"Ben doesn't have a clue what he's doing. I'll have a talk with him in the morning."

Jurgis tried not to look at him eat. "What do we do about Nick Thomas?"

"Oh, I don't think he'll be a problem. I checked him out. He has a checkered past."

"I'm surprised. That guy seems like a total straight arrow."

"Well, he isn't," Blaine said, shoveling another load of taro duck into his mouth.

Blaine Daniels' film noir collection of VHS tapes had long been replaced with DVDs. After dinner and back home, he put on a copy of *The Big Sleep* and opened a screenplay writing program on his laptop. In his spare time he had been writing his own film noir.

He usually had a movie running in the background while he wrote or polished his prose. He also studied the films for ways to enhance the bottom line of the company.

The script—complete, printed, and bound, was in the top desk drawer of his desk, but he couldn't help but fine-tune it.

Despite Blaine Daniels' natural pull to the wrong side of the law, he had avoided jail, although he was once brought up on fraud charges. A chain of evidence mixup got the charges dropped. Instead of serving as a warning, it emboldened him. He felt as though he could get away with anything.

And to him, making a film was a perfect way to launder money.

Chapter Thirty-Nine

The following morning Nick made his way north to Katherine's home in the Sea Cliffs district of San Francisco. It was a cool fall day, and Nick sat in the living room in front of the roaring fireplace. Katherine was in the chair opposite him, legs tucked under her. Nick had a cup of coffee on the table next to him.

"I can't thank you enough for what you did for me, Kathy, with *Icarus* and everything else."

From anyone else, being called 'Kathy' would rankle her. From Nick, it was endearing and made her feel warm inside. She was Kathy when they dated in college.

"You've thanked me enough. You've already paid me back, which I didn't want. My ex-husband destroyed you financially."

"And you have to let go of that. It wasn't your doing and you are not to blame." Nick took a sip. "It was wonderful to see *Icarus* pull into Honolulu. It felt like home to be back aboard."

"How is the old girl?"

"Good as new. I just put her back in the water. The ancient diesel engine finally called it quits, and I hauled *Icarus* out and put in a new one. Then I scraped the barnacles, put on a fresh coat of paint, and gave her a thorough cleaning. Willie helped me put in a second bilge pump. I also put in a wind turbine and an air conditioner."

He left out the part about Gretchen moving on board.

Katherine laughed when Nick talked excitedly about his boat. She wondered if she ever meant as much to him as *Icarus* did.

"Why are you laughing?" Nick asked.

"You and your boat. It's nice that it gives you such pleasure."

Nick looked at her sideways.

"How is Willie? He has a good heart. He was a big help to get *Icarus* to Hawaii."

"Willie is fine. He flew out with me. He's staying with his family here in the city. I'm meeting him for lunch."

"Please give him my regards."

"I will. I owe you two a lot and can't thank you enough."

They both took another sip of coffee.

"I met with John Mitchell," Nick said.

"John? Is everything all right? Has Lance been in touch with you? What's going on?"

"Lance has nothing to do with it. I wanted to get his read on something going on in Hawaii."

"Oh," Katherine said. "Do you ever wonder where Lance is?"

"Occasionally. I guess I've moved on from that," Nick replied.

"That's good. I've moved on as well," Katherine said. It was easier for her, she thought. She hadn't lost nearly everything, as Nick had.

"I wonder if he and Jody are still an item," Katherine said.

She cringed, realizing it might still be a sore spot for him. "I'm sorry. That was inconsiderate of me to ask."

Nick shrugged. "It's okay. As I said, I've moved on."

The sting of Lance and Jody running off with nearly everything he possessed had dulled. At that point in his life it was a story to tell, 'Cocktail party fodder,' as Jim would call it.

Nick turned back to the fire. They sat in comfortable silence and sipped their coffee. Their timing had been lousy since they first got together. When they dated in college, it was a summer romance, and their parents heard wedding bells when they did not. Since then, there was someone or something in the way of them getting together. They never talked about it and they didn't have to. It had always been painfully obvious.

Chapter Forty

After coffee with Katherine, Nick drove down Bush Street, past the Dragon Gate defining the entrance to Chinatown at Grant Avenue, and turned left on Kearny. He parked in the St. Mary's Square Garage.

Growing up in San Francisco, Nick knew this Chinatown, and something of its history. San Francisco began in Chinatown. Portsmouth Square in Chinatown was the location of the first private home and the first school in San Francisco, called Yerba Buena back then. Grant Avenue, leading into Chinatown, was the first street in San Francisco.

Willie's family had been in Chinatown for longer than most Californians, having come to the area for the gold rush. The first Chinese arrived in San Francisco in 1848. Two years later, 20,000 arrived in what they called *Gam Sann*—Gold Mountain.

Many came to California with the promise of striking it rich, finding a piece of the *Mother Lode,* and returning to their families wealthy beyond their dreams. The result turned San Francisco Chinatown into the largest Chinatown outside of Asia and the oldest in North America.

The Chinese, for the most part, were accepted in the gold

fields when surface gold was easy to find. When that changed, and competition for finding gold increased, so did animosity towards Chinese and other foreigners. Laws were passed, such as the Foreign Miners' Tax, which effectively pushed the Chinese out of the gold fields. Most Chinese were relegated to building the Transpacific Railroad or working menial jobs no one else was willing to do. Next came the Chinese Exclusion Act, which banned immigration from China to the US from 1882 to 1943. There were some exceptions for non-laborers, such as merchants, clergy, diplomats, teachers, and students.

Other Chinese who were, or claimed to be, children of American citizens, were allowed into the country. This led to "paper sons" and "paper daughters", those buying false documentation of family citizenship. They studied for months to pass the grueling immigration interrogation, which occurred at the Angel Island Immigration Station, situated in the San Francisco Bay.

The successful Chinese were the ones supplying goods and services to the miners, such as Willie's ancestors, who arrived in 1849.

When China allied with the US in World War II, the ban on Chinese immigration was repealed.

After the 1906 earthquake that leveled most of San Francisco, the buildings in Chinatown changed in style from Western and European to semi-Chinese. The new buildings had pagodas with curved Asian cornices perched atop traditional rectangular western architecture. To Nick, Chinatown in San Francisco looked older than most parts of Hong Kong.

To many non-residents, Chinatown is a tourist destination. It's more than that. Chinatown is well organized, with deep roots and traditions and powerful business and family ties. Even today, many families in Chinatown live together in Single Room Occupancy housing averaging eight by eight feet—cramped quarters for a family of four, even with a bath and kitchen down the hall. Like Chinatown in Honolulu, many residents lived below the poverty level. On Willie's visits to his San Francisco family in his youth, he ran with his cousins through the alleyways connecting the sub-districts of Chinatown.

Some established families were prosperous. Willie's uncle and aunt, for example, owned a four-story building on Grant Avenue. The ground floor was an antique store, the middle floors, apartments, and the top, the penthouse. Willie's aunt and uncle were away touring buildings to buy in Texas. Willie had the run of the place and ensconced himself in the penthouse apartment overlooking Saint Mary's Park and the financial district.

Nick rang the bell next to the antique store. A minute later, Willie opened the door.

He had a book in his hand, *Love in the Time of Cholera* by Gabriel García Márquez. Nick took a closer look—the book was the Spanish language edition.

"Come on up," Willie said, turning and climbing the stairs.

Nick followed Willie to the salon on the third floor.

"This place hasn't changed since I graduated from Berkeley," Willie said, on the way up.

It was a long room with a kitchen at one end and two bedrooms at the other. There were Chinese calligraphy prints on the walls, ancient Chinese inlaid chests, shelves of books in Chinese and English, a couch, and a rosewood dining table.

Willie plopped down on the couch. Nick sat at the other end.

"How did the business go?" Willie asked.

"Fine. I'm done with that."

Willie looked at his watch. "Are you hungry?"

Nick and Willie walked north on Grant Avenue, crossed California Street to Old Saint Mary's Cathedral and the Chinese Mission. There, they came upon the Green Street Mortuary Band leading a procession of a modern black convertible carrying a family. Those in the back seat propped up an enormous photograph of the deceased, framed in gold and boarded with white flowers.

The band was there to announce and pay tribute to the passing of the person and to make noise to scare away unfriendly spirits and open the road to their passing to the next plane. Two limousines took up the rear.

"I remember when it was a big old 1960s Cadillac convertible with the photograph that used to follow the band," Willie said as they stood on the corner and watched. The band, led by a woman playing the clarinet, wore black suits and ties with white shirts and white military-style hats. They were serious musicians who played in the band as a side gig. The group was an offshoot of the Cathay Boys Band formed in 1911, and originally composed of Chinatown residents, but now it was multi-ethnic with musicians coming from around the Bay Area.

"The music is said to help the deceased get to heaven faster while taking them on a final journey, through where they had been born and raised," Willie said.

When the procession passed, Willie and Nick crossed Commercial Street, turned right, and walked down to Kearny Street and down the stairs into the R & G Lounge.

"I've been dying to have their salt and pepper crab," Willie said.

"The last time I was here was with you when we were going to school," Nick said, looking around at the simple decor of wood walls and a mixture of wood and tile floors. "It hasn't changed much."

"And a lychee martini. I want a lychee martini," Willie said.

The waiter came and Willie ordered in Cantonese.

"I took the liberty of ordering for you," he said when the waiter left.

"I assumed."

"You'll love it."

"As long as it's not taro duck, I'm sure I will."

"The last time I was here was for a Red Egg and Ginger Party for my cousin's baby. I happened to be in town that weekend," Willie said.

"Red Egg and Ginger?" Nick asked.

"'Moon-yut' in Chinese. The tradition began when there was a horrible infant mortality rate in China. If the kid made it through the first month, the family planned a celebration to introduce the child to the family. These days a lot of people have the parties at the one year mark."

"That's like the one year baby luau they have in the islands," Nick said.

The waiter came by and delivered two lychee martinis. They raised their glasses, toasted, and took sips.

"Ah. That's nice," Willie said, then continued with his story. "Back then, it was when the kid was named, although now it's named when it's born."

"Why Red Egg and Ginger?"

"The egg is obviously a fertility symbol. White is a symbol for sorrow and death, so they are dyed red, a symbol of good luck and unity."

"And the ginger?" Nick asked, taking a sip.

"The ginger helps the mother bring her body back into balance after childbirth."

An enormous Dungeness crab and an equally large platter of vegetables arrived at the table.

"Now we're talking," Willie said, reaching for a crab leg.

The two of them attacked the food.

"This is fantastic," Nick said, adding more vegetables to his plate.

"Yeah," Willie managed, between mouthfuls.

The carnage continued until a good part of the crab had been devoured. Willie had done the most damage, judging by the pile of shells on each of their plates. Willie's capacity to ingest vast amounts of food and not show it amazed Nick.

Nick wiped his mouth with his napkin, folded it, and set it on the table.

Willie sat back in his chair and stifled a burp. "So. What's the plan?"

Nick reached for his water glass and took a sip. "I'll head back to Jim's tonight and catch the morning flight back to Honolulu. What about you?"

"I'm going to stick around for a while. I'll be back before we sail to Moloka'i."

Chapter Forty-One

"How is Willie?" Jim asked.

Nick left the city before traffic and was back at Jim's home.

"Willie's fine, as always."

"I thought we would eat light tonight. I made us a dinner salad."

"That sounds great. Willie and I had a huge lunch."

"That guy can really eat. I hope you didn't try to keep up with him."

"Not a chance."

"Do you miss it?" Jim asked, pouring wine into Nick's glass.

"You mean my past life on the West Coast? The money, the trappings, the cars, the plane, the houses, the business, the wife?"

"Yes, all of that."

"I'm not sure I ever got the chance to miss it. Life has been a whirlwind." Nick took a sip of wine.

"You don't seem to lack for excitement."

"The things are just things. The most important items we stored away in that spot up north—Family heirlooms, books, things like that. As for my wife, ex-wife — Jody, well, our marriage was falling apart. That, of course, had to do with her affair with Lance. I have to say that took me by surprise."

"You sure have been through a lot."

"I met this guy once. His house burned down with everything in it. Once he got over the initial shock, he said it was the most amazingly freeing experience," Nick said, taking a bite of salad.

"Is that how you feel?"

"To a great extent, yes. My life is much more simple than it was before Lance absconded."

"I have to say you look content, even though you are back in touch with the FBI."

Chapter Forty-Two

The next morning, Nick had cleared airport security when a man in a Hawaiian Airlines uniform approached him.

"Mr. Thomas?"

"Yes?"

"Hawaiian Airlines has chosen you for complimentary access to our Premier Club."

"That's nice, but Hawaiian Airlines doesn't have a Premier Club here at SFO."

"It's very private. If you'd follow me, sir."

The man led Nick down the concourse and stopped at an unmarked door.

Nick eyed the man. "This doesn't look like an airport lounge."

"It isn't. Special Agent John Mitchell would like a word with you."

"Why didn't you say so?"

The man entered a code into a box and held the door open for Nick. "Have a pleasant flight," he said, showing Nick in and leaving.

The room held only a table with four chairs around it.

Mitchell sat drinking coffee from a mug, a stainless steel thermos beside his cup. There was another empty cup on the table.

Mitchell stood up and put out his hand to shake.

"Thank you for pulling me out of harm's way yesterday. That guy was right. I would be dead if you hadn't moved so quickly."

Nick shook his hand. "I'm sure you would've done the same for me."

"Nevertheless."

Nick took a seat in one of the plastic chairs. "This feels like old times, teaming up to beat the bad guys at their own game."

Mitchell sat down. "We didn't beat the bad guy the last time we played, and the case is still open," he said as he unscrewed the lid to the thermos and poured Nick a cup.

"And I assumed I was no longer a suspect." Nick took a sip. It was good. Mitchell's coffee always was.

"Your company has generated interest at the FBI. In fact, I have been directed to assemble a task force to investigate it," Mitchell told him. He reached into his coat pocket and retrieved a mobile phone and handed it to Nick. "I want you to use this phone to contact me. It's encrypted and can only dial certain numbers, one of which is mine. You'll be meeting with an agent in Honolulu, if the situation warrants it."

Nick considered the phone in his hand. The events had escalated quickly. He put the phone in his pocket and stood up. "I've got a flight to catch."

"Call me anytime, day or night," Mitchell said, "And, Nick?"

"Yes?"

"I shouldn't have to tell you not to talk about this with anybody."

"I understand."

"Does anybody else know?"

"Jim Fujiyama," Nick replied.

"I'll have a word with him. Anyone else?"

"I've told no one else the company may be doing illegal things. A couple of friends have heard stories of how screwy it is. I learned long ago not to take my work home with me. I rarely discuss it once I leave the office."

"I wish I had learned to do that. It might have saved my marriage."

On the way to his plane, Nick thought about his meeting with Mitchell and when he reached the gate, he stopped at the agent's desk.

"Is there a seat available in first class?" he asked.

"Let me check." The agent clicked away at the computer. "Yes, we just had a cancellation. Would you like to upgrade?"

"Yes, please," Nick handed the agent his company credit card.

He might as well put dirty money to good use.

Chapter Forty-Three

The flight back from San Francisco landed without event, and Nick took a ride share from the airport back to the Ala Wai Harbor. As he walked down the dock to *Icarus,* he heard *Finlandia* by Jean Sibelius coming from the boat's stereo. The intense music assaulted Nick when he slid open the hatch. He entered the boat and found the air conditioner running, and Gretchen sprawled on the settee, reading intently, dressed in a pair of his boxers and his Honolulu Greek Festival T-shirt. Every flat surface in the saloon was piled high with books and papers. When he turned down the volume on the stereo, Gretchen leapt off the settee and spun around.

"Hi," Nick said.

"Oh, you startled me. I didn't think you would be back so soon." She started stacking and organizing her books and papers. "I had planned to have the boat neat and tidy and dinner ready for you when you arrived."

"I need to run into the office. I wanted to drop off my bags. How about I come back in a couple of hours?"

When he returned to the office, the place was buzzing. More investors had come and gone, some paying a return visit to invest more funds, others were new to Nick. The company had met payroll, as Blaine had promised. An investor came in at the eleventh hour and wired money to the company through yet another offshore bank, this one in Switzerland. Blaine had left for Florida to tour a defunct amusement park to buy.

Nick got caught up in his work and called Gretchen to tell her he would get back to the boat late. It was after eight o'clock when he arrived. Dinner was warming on the stove, and *Icarus* was spotless.

Chapter Forty-Four

The following Monday at the office, Claire arrived in a sunny mood, hands filled with fresh flowers. She had returned from a week-long trip to Dallas for a marketing conference.

"You're in a good mood," Nick said. "How did the convention go? Did you learn much?" As far as Nick could tell, Claire knew nothing about marketing, corporate policy, corporate structure, or the basics of running a business.

"Oh, yeah, that was okay. Kind of boring, actually. I met up with my old friend, Bart. We really hit it off. We spent my entire time in Dallas together."

"I guess you're done with your husband?"

"Oh, yeah. When he cheated on me with my friend—his secretary, it was over."

"What's Bart like?"

"He's great. He and his wife are old friends of mine. She wants to stay with him, but he's ready to move on. He hasn't been attracted to her for years. He wants to be with me now."

"How is that any different from what your husband did to

you with his secretary? Now you're the other woman." Once Nick blurted out the words, he instantly regretted doing so.

"What? It's not the same at all." She crossed her arms and glared at him.

"You're right. It's none of my business. I'm sorry."

He backed out of her office, disappointed in himself.

I've got to get out of here. I don't like who I'm becoming.

There was one bright spot in the company. Betty, the executive assistant, shared by all the directors, was unflappable, solid, and a joy to work with. She came in on time, exuded confidence, and kept the place running. She did everything from making coffee for Blaine to taking minutes at the board meetings; nothing was too big or too small a task. Occasionally she talked Blaine out of a few of his wilder ideas before they took root, such as buying an entire town not far from his hometown of Globe, Arizona. She saw Nick as the one to confer with regarding company matters.

"What does Claire do?" she once asked Nick.

"She's the Chief Marketing Officer."

"I know what her title is, but what does she do?"

"She's a friend of Blaine's," Nick said, as if it explained everything.

Betty nodded as if it did.

It was clear to Nick that Betty had worked for larger, more established organizations and at a higher level than at their company, although he had not read her resumé and wasn't aware of her background. When he asked her why she came to work for the company, she said, "I wanted something less stressful with regular work hours. I got tired of putting in twelve-hour days."

Betty saw the company as a playground for Blaine. There

were many occasions where Nick and Betty exchanged an eye roll, a smirk, or a shared glance of shocked disbelief during a staff meeting or other function.

As the days passed, Betty saw the tension grow in Nick, particularly after he returned from the mainland.

The company continued to expand, and Nick didn't recognize some people at the office. When he asked, Betty told him the staff count had grown to more than fifty. Blaine had negotiated with the landlord for additional space in the building, and they split the programs into two spaces, the medical billing on the first floor with the administrative office, and the digital graphics moved to a space on the second floor. It made Nick's work life even more chaotic, but gave him a lot of exercise going up and down the stairs. Blaine continued to take people off one project and put them on another. It caused chaos and messed with morale of the development teams.

When staff came to Nick complaining about being reassigned mid-task, Nick asked them to continue their work from their new desk and move back the next day. It became a joke to the programming teams. One enterprising programmer named Laura set up a betting pool on the potential changes. She wrote a computer program to track the bets. Those playing—everyone on the team—bet on who Blaine shifted and when. The payoff was each Friday before lunch, giving the winner a nice weekend bonus.

One morning Nick walked by Ben's office and stopped at his door. Ben usually arrived by nine-thirty, when Nick had already been in the office for more than an hour. He was sitting in front of his computer, back to Nick, staring at the screen, scratching his head, perplexed. He often mentioned to Nick he would rather play music or go to a strip club than sit at his desk.

Nick watched him for a moment. He had a pallor not common in Hawaii. Ben spent his days in the office and nights in clubs and bars.

Nick almost felt sorry for the guy. He was given a job he was untrained for, doing what Blaine told him to do, and given the least information possible. Nick saw Ben as a fall-guy, someone Blaine could blame if everything came crashing down.

He began to see himself in the same position.

The next morning, Nick spotted a fresh addition to the wall of Blaine's office. He stepped in and walked around the desk. It was a post-impressionistic oil painting of fruit on a tabletop in front of a window with a washbasin and glass. He was sure it was a Cézanne. But was it an original or a copy? He leaned forward and examined it. The painting had a brownish tint of age. The frame was dirty and looked ancient.

He took a picture of the painting with the burner telephone.

As he turned to leave, Nick glanced into the partially open drawer of Blaine's desk. A small handgun sat on top of a pile of papers. Nick took one more picture and left the office.

Chapter Forty-Five

Nick continued to get to the office early and plan meetings in the late mornings and afternoons. It limited his interaction with Blaine and the other board members, who continued to arrive at the office later and leave earlier. It gave Nick the opportunity to scan or photograph company documents and board meeting minutes. The trip to San Francisco to "cover his backside," as Jim put it, had turned Nick into an undercover agent.

He wasn't sure how he felt about it.

The next Monday, Blaine and Claire were traveling for the week and it was only Nick and Betty in the office.

"Where's Ben?" Nick asked Betty.

"He took the day off. He has a dentist appointment this morning and doctors' appointments this afternoon."

"I think I'll walk next door to the coffee shop. Can I bring you something back?"

"I'd love a large latte," she said, reaching for her purse.

"No, it's on me."

"Thanks."

When he returned, he dropped Betty's drink off at her desk.

"Anything exciting happen while I was gone?" he asked.

"No, thank goodness. No visitors, not even a phone call." When Nick entered his office, he saw a flash drive on the desktop that wasn't there when he left. Nick sat down and examined the device. *Betty said no one had come by.*

He took his personal laptop from the case beside his desk, turned it on, logged in, and turned off the wireless. He opened a program and plugged in the thumb drive to scan for viruses and trojans. In a minute, the program came back with a clean report.

Nick opened the drive and saw a group of file folders labeled *Investors*, *Transfers*, and *Projects*. When he opened a folder labeled *Transfers*, he found dozens of documents. Nick's eyes grew wide. It was the confirmation of money transfers to banks in Andorra, Panama, and Lebanon, besides the ones Nick knew of from Jamaica, Switzerland, and the Cayman Islands. He closed the files and ejected the thumb drive. He shut down his computer and closed the lid. The office was not the place to be looking at the files. He would wait until he was back on *Icarus* and alone.

Nick surveyed the room. He had not personalized it much. It was one upside of living on a boat; one can't acquire many possessions. He was glad he hadn't got too comfortable in his office.

Later that afternoon on *Icarus*, Nick used the encrypted mobile phone to call Mitchell and tell him of the flash drive full of files that appeared on his desk.

"Don't do anything with it. I'll get back to you tomorrow," Mitchell told him.

Thursday morning Betty appeared at Nick's office door.

"Big Jack is here to see you," she said.

"What about?" Nick. asked

"He wouldn't say. I put him in the conference room."

"Okay, thanks."

Big Jack kept to himself, and his coworkers found him to be arrogant and unpleasant. Nick met with him on Monday mornings as he did with his top programmers, but had never met with him at any other time. Nick got up and walked to the front office, taking with him a notepad and his fountain pen. He escorted Big Jack to the conference room and closed the door.

"What can I do for you?" Nick asked.

"You said if I ever need to talk to you, I could. So here I am."

Nick waited. Big Jack squirmed in his chair.

"I was reviewing the code for the medical billing software before I compiled it."

"Yes?"

"I found something," Big Jack said, squirming more.

"Go on."

"There are lines of code. I didn't put them in the program. I know every line of code in there."

"That's a lot of code," Nick said.

"Yeah, a million lines and growing. I have an ability—and I don't sleep much. The code's buried deep, but I found it."

"What do these lines of code that you didn't put in the program do?"

"It's complicated and very elegant."

"Can you tell me an uncomplicated version?" Nick pulled his notepad toward him in and uncapped his fountain pen.

Big Jack took a deep breath. "It skims money. Not much,

basically a floating point error, but it adds up. It adds up quickly."

Nick thought of Blaine at their first meeting. He talked about automating the billing software and making it more efficient.

"Go on."

"But it's more complicated than that. This is where the elegant part comes in. The skimming amount changes, making it harder to track. Whoever did it set the overage to go to a cryptocurrency money exchange. Those are places where you can buy and sell cryptocurrencies like Bitcoin. They probably have a person on the inside of the exchange who set up accounts that can't be traced. Once the money is in an exchange, they can move it around to other types of cryptocurrency that aren't regulated by the United States. It's kind of the Wild West out there."

It was time for Nick to take a deep breath. "Can you tell who added the code?"

"I can't. You know how Blaine keeps shifting people between projects? That obscures who worked on it. I can't tell who did it."

"Have you told anyone else what you found?"

"No, just you."

"Good, don't."

"If this goes live, it will be illegal. What are you going to do about it?"

"I'll take care of it."

Big Jack pushed back from the table. "I'll give you twenty-four hours, and then I'm going to talk to the authorities. I need to look after myself."

"I understand. Until then, you need to go back to work, act like it's business as usual." Nick checked his watch. "Let's meet here tomorrow morning at the same time. I will need your mobile number."

After the meeting with Big Jack, Nick returned to his office, grabbed his leather backpack, and stopped at Betty's desk.

"I'm going to take the day off, go to the beach," he told her.

"Good for you," Betty said.

Nick got into his Triumph and drove down the road past old Fort Ruger to Diamond Head. He drove through the tunnel and into the crater. Native Hawaiians called Diamond Head, a dormant volcanic tuff cone, *Le'Ahi*.

The lip of the crater resembled the dorsal fin of a tuna—*ahi* in Hawaiian. In the 1800s, the British mistook calcite crystals on the nearby beach for diamonds and the name *Diamond Head* stuck.

He took his backpack and headed up the trail and the first set of 74 steps, through a tunnel, up another 99 steps to another tunnel, and then climbed a spiral staircase until he arrived at the pillbox at the peak, a concrete lookout built during World War II. He caught his breath as he took in the views of the south shore of Oahu and Waikiki. It was a breezy and clear day and he tried to make out *Icarus* in her slip in the harbor. He moved away from the tourists and locals and took the encrypted phone from his backpack to call Mitchell, who answered right away. Nick told him what Big Jack had found in the software code.

"This Big Jack, can he be trusted?"

A gust of wind rocked Nick and he caught his balance.

"I assume he's not involved. He gave me twenty-four hours to do something about it or he is going to talk to the authorities. He doesn't want to get blamed for it."

Tourists came walking his way, and he moved away from them, further down the path.

"I've already contacted our local office in Honolulu and have been talking with a Special Agent there. His name is Leland Chan. I'll set up a meeting with you."

"All right. How do I get in touch with him?"

"Leave your encrypted phone on. He'll be in touch with you."

"Okay. But make it fast before Big Jack makes a mess of it. He's nervous."

"I will. One more thing," Mitchell said.

"Yes?"

"Some of these investors are big time bad guys, Nick."

"Terrific."

"Be careful. Watch your back."

An hour later, Nick drove down Interstate H-1 toward Sand Island, where the constant flow of container ships arrived after they steamed across the Pacific to deliver their cargo to the Hawaiian Islands. He turned the Triumph down a potholed side street and made his way to Keʻehi Lagoon and *La Mariana Sailing Club*. The club is home to a tiki bar and restaurant built in the 1950's as a dream of Annette La Mariana Nahinu and her Kiwi husband, Johnny Campbell. The club began with 13 slips for 13 boats and grew from there.

Nick parked his car and made his way down the shaded brick path, past the wood tiki carved posts between boat docks and into the club. He checked in at the door and a hostess guided him into the bamboo bar where a pony-tailed bartender with a white beard reaching to his chest served drinks with speed and efficiency. Several regulars sat at the bar—a mix of workers from Sand Island and nearby live-aboard sailors. Nick followed the hostess past the fishing floats and shell lamps hanging from the ceiling and more carved tikis to a booth in the back corner, away from other diners. A moment later, a man entered wearing dark slacks, polished shoes, and a blue and white patterned aloha shirt covered by a sport coat.

"Nick Thomas?"

Nick stood up. "Leland Chan?"

They shook hands and sat.

The waitress approached and they both ordered plantation iced tea—a mixture of iced tea and pineapple juice. They perused the menu and both chose the mahi-mahi sandwich.

"I understand you have something for me," Chan said.

Nick handed Chan the thumb drive.

"Your assistant gave this to you?"

"I didn't see who left it on my desk. I can only assume it was her. There was no one else in the office."

"Maybe I can get our people to lift a print." He pulled an evidence bag from his jacket and slid in the drive.

"She doesn't work for you, does she?" Nick asked.

"Your assistant, Betty Kanashiro? No. She checks out clean, though."

The waitress came with their order. They both ate in silence for a while.

"Willie says you're a Boy Scout," Chan said, sitting back and taking a sip of his iced tea.

"Willie? You know Willie?"

"I pulled your phone records and saw you two are often in contact."

"That figures, you pulling my phone records." Nick took a bite.

"Willie's my cousin."

"Of course he is," Nick said, shaking his head. "It's a small island."

"I told Willie not to ask you why I called him to check up on you. I'd prefer you don't discuss the details of the investigation with him."

"I understand."

They talked more about the company, Chan asking for more detail in lots of areas. It was clear to Nick that Chan had talked with Mitchell, had pulled records of the employees, and had done his homework.

"Do you see any standouts in the company, those exhibiting odd behavior?" Chan asked.

"Odd behavior? Between the incompetent and unqualified officers and directors, the company is a total nuthouse. It would be easier to tell you who acts normal."

"Keep your eyes open and tell me if there is anything you think I should know. For example, another thumb drive showing up on your desk. Can you unlock and hand me the mobile phone Agent Mitchell gave you?"

Nick punched in the passcode and handed the phone to Chan, who took it and entered a number.

"Now you can call me from this phone," he said, handing it back.

Driving back to his office, Nick wanted a diversion. The car was running well, the tires were new, and the sky clear. He got off at the Pali Highway exit and made his way around Punchbowl Crater, home to the National Memorial Cemetery of the Pacific. He drove up Tantalus Drive and the ten-mile loop of steep hills, hairpin turns, and the occasional head-on with a Japanese tourist in the wrong lane.

He stopped at the Tantalus Lookout where he could see from Diamond Head to Pearl Harbor. He surveyed the urban sprawl of

Honolulu. The place had changed in the years he had been coming to the island. The mom and pop stores were gone, replaced with ubiquitous big-box stores. When he was younger, visiting Hawaii with his parents, Nick remembered not being able to purchase many things on the island. That was no longer the case; there were nearly 350 stores at Ala Moana Shopping Center alone. It was early in the afternoon and he saw traffic piling up on the H1.

It was the same everywhere, Nick thought: You should have been here twenty years ago.

Early the next morning, Nick knocked on Big Jack's cardboard door.

"Enter," came the reply.

Nick poked his head in. "I'm taking you to lunch today. Be ready at eleven."

Big Jack looked at him over his glasses, nodded, and turned back to his computer.

Big Jack wedged himself into the passenger seat of Nick's Triumph. To get him to fit, they had to take the top down on the car. Nick had barely enough room to shift gears. Big Jack took it in stride and made no complaints.

As Nick made the turn on to Kapiolani Avenue, Big Jack asked, "Where are we headed?"

"You'll see."

Nick turned left onto McCully Street, past the convention center, and over the Ala Wai Canal.

"Waikiki? No one goes to Waikiki except tourists."

"Yes, it will be an excellent place for a private, uninterrupted meeting."

It looked comical, Big Jack overflowing from the car, it listing to starboard as they turned left onto Kalākaua Avenue. As they crossed Saratoga Avenue and entered the heart of Waikiki, Big Jack, wide eyed, moved his head from side to side, looking at the shops, hotels, and tourists.

They came to a stoplight and a Japanese tourist moved forward to take a picture of the men in the little black car. Big Jack smiled and gave the photographer a *shaka* sign.

After the light turned green, Nick continued down the road.

"If we run into anyone either of us knows, I am taking you to lunch to thank you for the outstanding work you are doing," Nick said.

"Got it."

Nick pulled into the porte-cochère at the Moana Surfrider, one of the oldest and grandest hotels in Waikiki. Big Jack extracted himself from the car with surprising agility. The valet took the keys and handed Nick a ticket. He turned it over. On the back was written:

Sixth Floor
Diamond Head Lanai

The small old brass elevator barely had room for the two of them. Nick winced when he heard the groan and felt the shudder from the mechanism as they ascended. On the sixth floor, they walked out onto the lanai, a place usually reserved for intimate weddings and private parties. A table with three chairs and a large cart with a buffet of bread, cold cuts, salad and fruit took up one corner. White cloth napkins were draped over what Nick assumed were cameras in the corners of the lanai. He walked to the railing and peered down at Waikiki beach and the tourists below. When he turned around, Leland Chan was standing in the doorway. He walked forward and shook Nick's hand. He turned, "Big Jack, I presume?"

"That's me."

They shook hands.

"Special Agent Leland Chan. Why don't we have lunch and have a talk. We can order off a menu if this doesn't suit you."

Big Jack perused the buffet. "I'm good, but you guys better go first."

After they finished lunch, Big Jack sat back in his chair and turned to Leland Chan. "I want anonymity and full protection. I did some digging and traced where the money was sent. It's going to a cryptocurrency exchange. They tried to hide it, but I'm smarter than they are. I have skills."

"I don't want you to do anymore digging on your own. If they get wind of it, you might tip them off," Chan said.

"I told you, I'm smarter than they are. They'll never find out."

Chan realized he wasn't getting through to him. "I'm sure you are smarter, however, you will not jeopardize or further interfere with this investigation." He paused for effect and leaned forward looking Big Jack in the eyes. "Do I make myself clear?"

Big Jack bristled, unaccustomed to being told what to do or not do. He puffed himself up. "I still want protection. I'm not part of that group and I don't want anything to do with them." He pulled a flash drive out of his pocket and slid it across the table. "It's encrypted." He took a piece of paper out of his trouser pocket and handed it to Chan. "Here's the passcode."

Nick looked at the two men squaring off across the table.

"Did you get enough to eat?" Nick asked Big Jack, hoping to break the tension.

Later that afternoon, Nick and Chan were back at *La Mariana,* seated in the booth.

"Big Jack is unhappy to be put on the sidelines of the investigation. He wants to do it all himself. Is he going to be a problem?" Chan asked.

"I don't know. Maybe." Nick looked past the foliage and to the docked boats. The rhythmic clanking of a halyard against a mast intruded on his thoughts.

"Probably."

Nick reached into his pocket, pulled out a flash drive, and handed it to Chan. "A few of Blaine's new investments. Look at the photo of the painting. It looks like an original Cézanne."

"A Cézanne painting? This is turning out to be a very interesting case."

"The surprises just keep on coming," Nick said.

"I didn't have time for a close look, but the files on the drive Big Jack gave me are very detailed."

"He's the best programmer in the company, and an eccentric." Nick told him about the office he made of cardboard.

"A cardboard office? Yeah, I'd call that eccentric."

"There's one more thing," Nick said.

"What's that?"

"Blaine Daniels has a handgun in his office desk drawer. There's a picture of that on the flash drive."

"Good to know."

Chapter Forty-Six

Across the Pacific in the hills of the Silicon Valley in the town of Los Altos, Raphael Sanchez sat in a sunny spot on his patio outside the French doors of his simple and elegant office. He sipped a cup of tea and thought about the company in Hawaii.

Sanchez, an underworld boss, expanded his influence through careful planning, software automation, solid business and management principles and, when necessary, violence and intimidation. Sanchez dabbled in anything profitable, but made most of his money in the drug trade. He made a point of insulating himself from all but his business operations and therefore had not met or communicated with Blaine Daniels.

Darby Jurgis came to Sanchez with a business proposition for a novel approach to automating medical billing. When Sanchez had him investigated, he found Jurgis had graduated from the lowest ranking accredited law school in the country. One of Sanchez's drug distributors paid his tuition to have his own in-house lawyer. He figured one law degree was as good as another. When Jurgis approached Sanchez, he had finished working off his tuition debt.

Jurgis presented Sanchez with a business concept which included Blaine Daniels as the CEO and overall software engineer. Jurgis had met Daniels when Daniels had run up a gambling debt with Jurgis's client. Rather than take a traditional route of breaking Daniels' bones, Jurgis' boss had put Daniels' software coding skills to work for his illicit business. Blaine Daniels, too, had worked off his debt. He had taken to the criminal world like a villain in the *film noir* movies he enjoyed so much.

Like many people residing in the United States, Raphael Sanchez felt the healthcare system was inefficient, overpriced, dominated by insurance companies and their lobbyists, and due for a complete overhaul. Until that happened, he was happy to profit from the broken bureaucracy, and put his drug profits into a legitimate business. Sanchez listened to Jurgis present his proposal of his medical billing software and concluded his idea had merit.

"Why Hawaii?" Sanchez had asked Jurgis when he finished his presentation.

"Blaine Daniels met a woman in Vegas and followed her to Hawaii. He's on his fourth marriage. It's hard to believe that guy can attract a woman; he's a total slob," Jurgis said.

Sanchez looked him up and down. He had a hard time believing Jurgis could attract a woman, either.

"Daniels has settled in and is ready to go," Jurgis said.

Sanchez thought about it. It would be good for the business not to be in his backyard, to put distance between his illicit operations and another legitimate one. Besides, all one hears about Hawaii is beaches, tropical breezes, palm trees, and the occasional hurricane. Yes, Hawaii may work.

"I am interested," Sanchez told Jurgis. "But I want a solid business plan."

Raphael Sanchez, impressed with the business plan he received, sent colleagues from the East Coast to Hawaii to invest in the company. They used several offshore accounts to obscure the source of the funds. His colleagues also gave him feedback on the operations of the business. Sanchez didn't like what he heard.

He had told Jurgis to keep the company at a low profile, but Blaine Daniels got caught up in the flash and glamor of the money. He had even started a digital graphics project, a passion of his. Sanchez wanted him focused on where the real money was to be made, the medical billing software.

Upon further investigation, Sanchez found Daniels was using the company as his own personal playground and had turned the potentially legitimate company into a way to skim profits and launder money for others. Sanchez had perfected plenty of ways to launder money. He did not want or need another of which he had no control, or one bringing him undue attention.

To make it worse, Blaine Daniels was sloppy and on a buying streak of real estate, art, gemstones, yachts, and other typical money laundering assets. Sanchez was told he was looking at amusement parks and European castles.

Sanchez's contacts in law enforcement were getting rumblings about the company being investigated for money-laundering. Blaine's outrageous purchases had drawn attention. To top it off, Blaine Daniels was messing with emeralds. Sanchez's Columbian counterparts viciously protected their spot in the emerald market, and he had no intention of angering them.

Sanchez sat back and considered the money he had put into

the project. Jurgis should be monitoring the company and was not doing his job. He was the only one tying Sanchez to the venture. Raphael Sanchez took one last sip of tea, picked up a burner mobile phone and called Rémi, his second-in-command.

It was time to cut his losses.

Chapter Forty-Seven

The following Friday, the crew assembled at Willie's home for the sail to Maui with a stop in Moloka'i. They then scattered in a last-minute provisioning frenzy.

Helena and Charlotte wanted fruit, and with an edict of "No damn bananas" from Willie, they left for a nearby grocery. Nigel took advantage of the time to forage for "tolerable whisky". Nick stayed behind, inspecting the boat before the sail across the channel.

The crew trickled back to the boat, and Caprice cast off from the dock at sunset. They made Makapu'u Point by 10:00 p.m. Beating upwind, they headed into the often treacherous Moloka'i Channel. Three miles offshore, the trade winds dropped, requiring them to start the "iron wind" and motor across the channel. There was excitement about the sea voyage until around midnight, when one-by-one the crew nodded off.

"Get some rest," Willie said. "I'll call you for the four a.m. watch."

"Okay." Nick moved to the bow away from the engines, leaned back into the foresail, and lay down on the foredeck. The sea was like glass.

In what seemed to him like only minutes, Nick woke to a tap on his shoulder. He followed Willie back to the cockpit, his path illuminated only by the waning full moon. Willie slipped through the companionway and into the bunk with Helena.

The engines chugged away with no city lights and a sky exploding with stars, an experience only exceeded, perhaps, if they were under sail. A perfect time, Nick felt, to consider his life in the universe. He questioned his luck. Ever since Lance had embezzled from him, his life had been a rollercoaster of craziness. He was born with a fortune and lost a fortune. He had a wife and lost a wife. What started as an interesting job turned into a money-laundering Ponzi scheme medical billing fraud nightmare.

Alone at the helm at sea, he was considering a drastic life change, but had no idea what it should be.

The engines droned on. Every few minutes he checked the compass and adjusted course. The uninhabited southwestern tip of Moloka'i off the port beam loomed as a shadow. Nick soaked up the starlight, gaining comfort from their steady glow. So it went, he and the stars, the moon, and the sea.

The GPS beeped, letting Nick know they were nearing their first stop. He woke Willie, who joined him in the cockpit and took the wheel. The draft on *Caprice* was slightly more than four feet. Willie knew the reef well, and Nick had no intention of running aground. There were a few times when Nick was onboard when the owner, sometimes, through no fault of his own, damaged his boat. "I'm glad I wasn't at the helm," was whispered among the crew.

One rule of sailing is *let the owner break his own boat.*

Willie stood at the helm and motored toward the reef. They dropped an anchor and a backup anchor and took the tender with their gear and crew to shore. Charlotte and Tina were behind on their schoolwork and planned on using the time to catch up. They volunteered to stay onboard as anchor watch.

As he motored to the shore, Willie told the crew, "In the 1920s my great-grandfather was living in Chinatown. He won this waterfront shack on Moloka'i in a game of *fan tan.* Our family has used the place as a get away ever since."

Later Nick asked Willie, "Did I ever tell you how my grandfather won *Icarus* in a poker game?"

"You did. Can you imagine what it would've been like if they hung out together? They would've been a riot," Willie said.

The "shack", maintained and updated by Willie's family, was a square room with large barn-like doors opening out toward the water. Inside were beds and bunk beds capable of sleeping ten. The structure was built from a mixture of native koa, ohia, and mango wood—whatever was available at the time. A kitchen and bathroom were at the back of the house. The crew spread out and chose their bunks. They planned to leave early the next morning for Lahaina.

While others hitched-hiked into Kaunakakai, the main town sixteen miles away, Willie retrieved a chess set in a carved wood box from a cupboard. Nick and Willie walked down to a picnic table by the shore and set up the game. Nick examined the chess pieces.

Kū, the Hawaiian god of war, represented the King.

Pele, goddess of the volcanoes, fire, lightning, and wind, was used as the Queen.

Lono, the god of agriculture and peacetime, was the Knight.

Kāne, the god of creation, sunlight, forests, and fresh water, was the Bishop.

Kanaloa, the god of the sea realm, was the Rook.

They were exquisitely carved. Nick thought they belonged in the Bishop Museum in Honolulu.

They played *Jankenpo*—the Hawaiian Pidgin English name for *Rock, Paper, Scissors,* to decide who would have the first move.

Nick kept his fist closed and played rock. Willie opened his hand flat and played paper, covering Nick's rock, winning the first move.

"How's it going with the company with the stupid logo?" Willie asked, opening with a pawn.

"Now Blaine wants to buy an amusement park," Nick replied.

"What happened to the castle?"

"I think he's still going to buy that." Nick moved a pawn.

"What ever happened with Herbert Jin, the guy I sent you to see about the gemstone?"

"Nice guy. I understand why you think of him as 'the professor'," Nick said.

"What were you doing with the gemstone?" Willie asked.

"I can't talk about it."

"Does this have to do with that company my cousin told me not to talk to you about?"

"I can't talk about it."

The game continued and Willie moved his King's Knight to

the King's-Bishop-three position. Nick focused on the chess-board. In all the years he had known Willie, they had never played chess.

Nick recognized the four-move checkmate gambit—known as the "Scholar's Mate". The problem with using such a tactic is if your opponent knows what you are doing and responds appropriately, he can take control of the board.

You could learn much about a person playing chess. Willie's mouth held a cocky smirk. Willie was so cocksure of himself Nick couldn't resist cleaning the board with him. What are friends for if not to keep you in line?

Willie took it well, but passed on a rematch.

"Maybe we should stick to backgammon," Nick said.

They headed back to the house to prepare lunch.

The next morning they continued to Maui where Willie planned to stay the week. The rest of the crew needed to get back to Honolulu for work and school. As planned, they would return the following weekend for the race back to Oahu.

A friend of Willys offered to take the crew to the airport, and at four that afternoon, they piled in the back of his truck for a ride across the island.

Chapter Forty-Eight

That afternoon when Nick arrived back at *Icarus*, he noticed a man parked in a nondescript Ford sedan near the boat. He had been around the marina for a couple of days before Nick left for Moloka'i.

Once onboard, Nick unpacked his seabag and called Chan.

"He's one of ours," Chan said.

"Why?"

"Just in case."

"In case what? Am I in danger?"

"I'd like you to meet me tomorrow," Chan said. "I can tell you more then."

The next morning, Nick Thomas sat shirtless while an FBI agent taped a microphone to his chest.

"How did it come to this?" Nick asked.

He was on the second floor of the Wo Fat building on the corner of Hotel and Maunakea streets in Chinatown. Wo Fat Restaurant had been Hawaii's oldest and had been operating for

123 years when it closed, and was the namesake of the villain in the "Hawaii Five-o" television series. The top floor had since been a gallery and nightclub and the ground floor converted to a Chinese market. The windows had been painted black from its time as a nightclub and colorful woodwork had also been painted over. After the nightclub closed, plans were underway to bring back a restaurant and add a small hotel. The restaurant is gone, but the Wo Fat sign is still there. The restaurant floor was huge and businesslike, not at all like its ornate exterior.

Nick looked around at the space. "And why are we in Wo Fat?"

"I don't want you to be seen going in or out of an FBI office. I called in a favor," Chan said.

"Can't I set my iPhone to record?" Nick asked, buttoning his aloha shirt—palm trees and sailboats, one of his favorites.

"It's too obvious," Chan said, "and it's not as if we expect them to search you. This isn't exactly a sophisticated lot."

"What if they *do* try to search me?"

"If anything goes wrong, get out. Just get up and leave. We will be listening and will be ready to move if necessary."

Nick glanced out the window. It had been a rare cool fall morning, with a low cloud hanging over Chinatown.

"Strange weather," he said.

Chapter Forty-Nine

Around 10 o'clock that morning, Nick was back in the office. He sat at the conference table with Blaine Daniels, Ben, and another potential investor who Daniels introduced as "Mike". Mike was from Hawaii, and it was the first time, to Nick's knowledge, an investor didn't come from out of state.

Ben sat quietly, looking beat down and sheepishly at Daniels, as if awaiting instructions. Daniels ignored him.

Nick gave Mike his standard talk about the company and its potential. When he was done, Blaine Daniels leaned forward and spoke.

"So Mike, if you invest in our company, we can take your investment and use it to buy a non-controlling interest in your company."

Nick's eyes grew wide. He cleared his throat. "Excuse me. What company would that be?"

Mike turned to Nick. "My partners and I own Coconut Joey's, the nightclub in Waikiki."

Nick struggled to maintain his composure. *Now it's a nightclub. That can't be good.* He knew nightclubs were cash businesses, often with dubious reputations. If something bad happened in Honolulu, it surprised no one when it happened at a nightclub. He tried to recall if he had heard anything about Coconut Joey's. He had often driven by it on the way to *Icarus*.

Nick felt a trickle of perspiration roll down his chest. It stopped where the tape held the microphone in place. He tried not to squirm in his seat and wondered what Leland Chan and his associates, listening in, thought of Blaine Daniels' new investment scheme.

Blaine Daniels registered Nick's discomfort and could tell he didn't like the nightclub investment. He already listened to him complain about the castle, amusement park, and the boat.

He had reached his limit.

Daniels turned to Ben. "Have Darby put together the paperwork. Let's get this done by the end of the week," he said, as if the meeting was merely a formality. He stood and offered a handshake to Mike. "I've got to head home and pack for another trip," he said, turning and walking from the room.

Nick returned to his office and retrieved his daypack.

"I have errands to run. I'm going to do that and get lunch and be back in a couple of hours," he told Betty on the way through the door.

When he got to his car, he called Chan. "We're done for the day. Daniels is heading home."

"We heard. I'll meet you back at Wo Fat."

Nick made his way downtown, taking side streets and cutting through neighborhoods. He looked in the rearview mirror to check if he was being followed.

I must be getting paranoid. Of course I'm paranoid; I'm an undercover agent for the FBI, and I have a microphone taped to my chest.

Paranoid or not, he parked the car three blocks away from the building, and to further cover his tracks, stopped in to a Chinese cooking store and bought a box of chopsticks. He saw a rear door and, leaving that way, headed back to Wo Fat.

Chan arrived before Nick, and Nick stood while the FBI technician removed the microphone and transmitter.

"You might want to get in the shower or the ocean and soak off the rest of that tape," the technician said.

Nick put on his shirt and joined Chan on the other side of the room.

"What did you think of Blaine Daniels' latest?" Nick asked, standing at the doorway.

"Come in and have a seat. I'm talking with John Mitchell in San Francisco." Chan pushed the speaker button on his phone and set it on the desk.

"Hello Nick, I understand you went undercover today," Mitchell said.

"Hi, John. Yes, and I still have tape on my chest to show for it."

"I've been catching Agent Mitchell up on today's operation," Chan said. "We've been looking at Coconut Joey's nightclub in Waikiki for almost a year. It's a front and money laundering operation for one of the local gangs."

"This guy Daniels sure isn't concerned who his business partners are," Mitchell said.

"It's like they are laundering money for each other, passing cash back and forth," Nick said, sitting down.

"We have been trying to find the source of the funds Blaine Daniel is receiving for investment. The money comes from different offshore accounts owned by shell companies.

We will probably never get to the bottom of that," Mitchell said.

"The guys from Coconut Joey's are not as careful as Daniels, and they have direct ties to organized crime in the islands," Chan said.

"Now that Blaine Daniels is receiving investment funds for them and taking part ownership in that venture, it makes our case much stronger," Mitchell said. "The subpoenas, search warrants, and indictments are being prepared. It's a complicated case with dozens of targets. The San Francisco and Honolulu offices are working to pull it together."

"Well, work fast. I think Blaine Daniels has lost patience with me questioning his investments," Nick said.

"Hold on a while longer. We are almost ready to move," Mitchell said.

"There's one thing I don't understand," Nick said.

"What's that?" Mitchell and Chan asked in unison.

"If Blaine Daniels just builds and runs the medical billing software without skimming money and makes a legitimate business out of it, it will be a tremendous success. Why mess with a good thing?"

"It's in his nature," Mitchell said.

Chapter Fifty

"I am really getting sick of that guy," Blaine said.

He and Darby Jurgis sat in Blaine's office later that afternoon. Jurgis had his feet up on the corner of Blaine's desk.

"I assume you're referring to Nick Thomas," Jurgis said.

"Of course I am. That guy is questioning my every move."

"Should he be?"

"What do you mean by that?"

"You are all over the map. You could rein it in a bit," Jurgis said, leaning forward.

"You, too? You're going to question me, too?"

"Yes, I am. You're going to draw undue attention to the company," Jurgis said. "Don't forget who made this happen. You wouldn't be here if it weren't for me."

"No, I won't. I know what I'm doing, as long as Nick Thomas stays out of the way."

Chapter Fifty-One

"You always smell spicy—like clove, vanilla, and ginger," Gretchen said, taking a sniff. "What is that?" she asked. "It's an old-fashioned scent. I like it."

They were curled up in the forepeak, her head on his chest. The weather had become hot and humid, and Nick had taken to staying on board in the air conditioning.

"It's Bay Rum. My father wore it and my grandfather wore it. I found an old bottle of it onboard in the engine compartment."

She took another sniff and sighed. "I've fallen in love with you."

"Really?"

"Yes, really. Why is that so hard to believe?"

"You've been preoccupied with your studies. I didn't think you gave us much thought," Nick said. It struck him how shallow their relationship was. They were two lonely people who connected, but it wasn't enough.

"Well it's true. I've fallen in love with you."

"That's nice," Nick said, kissing the top of her head. "Although you don't sound very enthusiastic."

"I don't want to be in love with you."

Nick turned his head and studied the ceiling of the cabin. "What's wrong with being in love with me?"

Gretchen sat up and leaned back against the bulkhead. "It will make my life complicated. I don't want that. I need to finish school, then go somewhere, it could be anywhere, for a residency."

"That's a year away."

"What are you going to do, follow me to wherever I get accepted, park there for the years it will take me to finish, and then follow me to wherever I get a full-time position?"

"I see your point." Nick knew she was driven and nothing or no-one would get in the way of her achieving her goals. Her decisiveness reminded him of his ex-wife, Jody.

"I don't want to be the one standing between you and your goals," Nick said.

"Sorry for being direct. I thought you should know."

She lay back beside him and ran her fingertips across the top of the cabin.

"I'm glad you told me before we got too far down the road," Nick said. He didn't relish the idea of getting emotionally involved with Gretchen, only to have her end it when she needed to leave to pursue the next step in her career.

Gretchen lay quietly for a moment.

"What do we do now?" she asked.

It was Nick's time to think. Her need to achieve her goals solved one of his more complicated dilemmas. The stakes had risen in the *Blaine Game*—as he now thought of it. Gretchen knew nothing of Nick's job or his involvement with the FBI. He wanted to keep it that way. There was a black car parked nearby watching over him. Blaine Daniels was now known to have bona fide connections to organized crime. John Mitchell told him these were "big time bad guys" and for him to "watch his back". He had never known Mitchell to be heavy on the hyperbole.

He didn't want Gretchen to be at risk by being with him. The whole situation was blowing up, and Nick wanted Gretchen off the boat and out of range.

And he couldn't tell her why.

He took a breath.

"We need to back off before one or both of us gets hurt," Nick said.

"What does that mean?" Gretchen asked, turning to him.

"It means we should stop seeing each other sooner than later."

"What do you mean by 'sooner than later'?"

Nick considered the investigation and how it was progressing. The sooner the better was right. He gave a shudder that Gretchen clearly noticed.

"I think we should stop spending time together by Friday, the day I fly to Maui."

"Friday? This Friday?" She sat up. "Why wait?"

She got up and tromped to the saloon.

He heard her gathering her things and shoving them into her book bag.

He knew nothing he could say or do to make the situation better. He gave her space and stayed in the forepeak cabin. She left in less than five minutes, placing the keys to the gate and the boat on the table.

It was awkward, and Nick felt miserable, but he knew it was the right thing to do.

After Gretchen left, Nick felt the hollowness inside him returning, coupled with a profound sense of relief that Gretchen would be one less concern for him.

He found her behavior odd, considering he never felt Gretchen committed to their relationship. She seemed more attracted to the quiet place to study—*Icarus,* than to Nick as a person. To him, the entire relationship was fraught with mixed messages. "Sometimes a girl wants to be pursued" followed by "I don't want a physical relationship." Once he was comfortable with that, she crawled naked into his bunk and climbed on top of him.

Next she told him she was falling in love with him but didn't want to, telling him they have no future. Then she stomped off in a huff when he suggested they end it before one of them gets hurt.

Trying to understand it was giving him a headache, and being honest with himself, the relationship was shallow and passionless. They were two lonely people needing or wanting company, and little else.

Chapter Fifty-Two

Around eight a.m. on a Friday morning, when Nick entered the office door, Betty was sitting at her desk.

"They're waiting for you in the conference room," she said.

"Who's waiting for me in the conference room?"

"Everybody. Blaine, Ben, Claire, Darby Jurgis—everybody."

"Any idea what's on the agenda?"

"With that crowd? Who knows? They have been talking quietly among themselves since seven this morning."

"They've been here since seven? Even Claire? She told me she doesn't like to get out of bed until after nine."

"They're all in there."

"They are going to have to wait," Nick said, heading to his office.

"Good for you," Betty called after him.

In his office, Nick pulled his laptop out of his backpack and put it on his desk. He opened it to the letter he had written the night before and read it once again. He sent the file to the printer in Betty's office, took a file folder out of a drawer, and walked down to retrieve the printout.

Betty had it in her hand by the time Nick got to her office.

She cocked her head and he saw a range of expressions cross her face as she handed him the paper.

He took the paper, pulled a pen from the holder on Betty's desk, signed the document, and slid it into the folder.

"Thank you, Betty. You are a treasure," he said, and walked down the hall to the conference room.

Nick opened the door and looked into the room. One empty chair at the round table faced the window, leaving Blaine back-lit and in shadow. Jurgis sat to his right and Claire to his left. Ben sat beside Jurgis.

"Betty said you were waiting for me."

"Have a seat, Nick," Blaine said.

"Sure." Nick sat down in the chair, setting the file folder on the table.

The harsh morning glare made Nick's eyes water. He squinted across the table.

Seeing Blaine smile at his reaction, Nick pulled sunglasses from his pocket, put them on, and smiled back at Blaine.

"There are defects in both of the projects," Blaine launched in.

"The projects are fine and they are on time and under budget. I'm not sure what defects you're talking about," Nick said. "Can you give me an example?"

Blaine leaned forward. "The code is incorrect in the input section of the billing software."

Nick also leaned forward, his eyes dark behind the sunglasses. "Yes, I told you it was incorrect and needed to be corrected to avoid problems down the line. You overrode me and told me to leave it as it is, that it doesn't affect how the program works. Which is true, for now. So we left it the way it was."

"It's wrong and you should have fought me harder to correct it. You're in charge of the projects, and you're responsible for defects in the projects."

"Ah," Nick said, "I see."

In fact, it made no sense and he did not see the point. Unless the point was to make him the fall guy.

Nick looked around the table at the other board members. They looked away—except Jurgis. He held Nick's gaze with a bland stare.

Nick recognized it as a cheap plot put forward by Blaine to get him out of the company. He was tired of Nick questioning his every move, even though he had tried to back off. The others followed along with anything Blaine said.

Nick considered Jurgis across the table, silhouetted in the morning light, unable to get a read on him. He was allied with Blaine and Nick had often seen them talking quietly in Blaine's office. Jurgis offered little and sat quietly through all the meetings. He wasn't a director of the company, but Blaine made sure the board meetings did not begin without him. Nick still saw Jurgis as the one in control.

Nick sat at the table, passively taking in the others. The sunglasses helped.

Jurgis studied his ragged fingernails. Blaine looked back at Nick, moist eyes blinking slowly like a lizard. He reminded him of Zeke. But Zeke wasn't an amoral narcissistic wannabe bad boy.

Ben drummed a pencil on the table until Claire reached over and took it away from him.

Nick sat back and waited.

Blaine broke the silence. "The board would like your resignation."

Nick turned his head to scan the crowd. Unhurried, he opened the file folder in front of him and took the paper out. He turned it to face Blaine and slid it across the table to him.

"Here you go," he said. Blaine's eyes got enormous. "I can tell you aren't happy with my work."

Nick waited two beats before he stood up, turned, took off his sunglasses, and walked back to his office. He heard a commotion from the conference room; everyone talked at once.

When Nick arrived at his office, he sat down in his chair and let out a breath, feeling a profound sense of relief. Being asked to resign was better for him and less suspicious than quitting, even with his resignation letter prepared.

He got up and retrieved a file box from the corner of his office. There wasn't much to pack. He left the desk lamp he bought at a thrift store down the street for the next occupant, packed a ruler, a rolled up dry erase board he stuck to the wall, and sweaters he wore in the over-air-conditioned offices into a box. He put his laptop in his leather daypack.

Betty came into his office with another box full of folders.

"These are copies of the company records, including the minutes from the board of directors' meetings. I've had them ready for you. You should take these with you," she whispered.

"Thanks. You're a marvel," Nick said, taking the box and setting it on his desk.

She moved forward and gave him a hug. "You be careful now," She turned and left the room.

It was an odd thing to tell someone who had just resigned.

Nick had just finished packing when there was a knock on his door.

Laura, the programmer who ran the betting pool, stood in the doorway.

"What happened? Ben came running into the office and said you resigned."

"Yes. It's time for me to move on. There's nothing else I can do here."

"Well, that sucks," she said.

"You know more about the two programs than anyone else. You may be taking over managing the teams. I'm sure you can handle it with no problems." Nick put the lids on the boxes.

"With Blaine continually moving people around on the programs? It's going to be a nightmare. I'm surprised you lasted this long."

"I'm sure you'll do your best."

Nick glanced out at his Triumph parked on the street directly out his window. He would have to walk all the way through the building, out the front door, around the building, and down the side to get to his car. It was only 20 feet from where he stood.

Nick stacked the boxes by the window and opened it.

"I'll go around and stand outside and you can hand them to me," Laura offered.

"Thanks, that would be great."

Nick took one last look around the office as Laura made her way to the outside.

When Laura appeared at the window, Nick handed the boxes to her.

"That's everything," Nick said.

Nick looked at the window and then at Laura.

"Oh, you have to do it," Laura said.

Nick nodded and hoisted himself through the window.

He carried the boxes to his car and loaded them onto the passenger seat. When he got behind the wheel, his mobile phone rang and he checked the caller ID.

"Hi, Joe," he said.

"I need some consulting for my underwater navigation system. I heard you were working for a new company, so I don't know if you'll have the time."

"Oh no, I'm free."

"Okay, can you come work for me, in say, two weeks? I should have funding by then."

"Sure. Let's talk after the holiday."

Nick got in the car among the boxes. The programming staff gathered on the sidewalk to give Nick a sendoff. Nick looked over at his office window. Blaine, Claire, and Ben peered out at the sight.

Nick started the car, put it in gear, and drove off, waving to his staff as he passed them.

"I don't know what we're going to do without Nick Thomas," Laura said to the others. "He was the only one in the front office who made any sense."

There was a murmur of agreement from the programmers.

When he got back to *Icarus*, Nick turned on the air conditioner, sat down and called Leland Chan.

"I was asked to resign, so I did," Nick said when Chan answered.

"That's a relief, and your timing is good. I was going to suggest you get out of there somehow."

"I had my resignation letter ready to go. I think I surprised them."

"We need to meet so you can give me the details," Chan said.

"Good idea. I have a box of company records that might be of interest."

"Can you meet me at La Mariana?"

"Sure. I can leave now."

"When we are done, you need to lie low," Chan said.

"I'm scheduled to fly to Lahaina tonight for Race Week, spend the weekend there, and sail back on Monday."

"Good. Things are about to get serious."

Chapter Fifty-Three

That morning an American Airlines flight from Phoenix arrived in Honolulu. On board the plane in the economy section was a couple from a small town outside of Durango, Colorado. They were the most anonymous couple imaginable. They talked blandly, walked blandly, and were bland looking. Their faces held neutral expressions and they didn't smile. Their clothes were of muted tones. They worked at being forgettable.

The couple booked a package deal which came with round-trip airfare, rental car, and a week at a Waikiki Hotel. When they got off the plane, they avoided the flower lei greeting, and with only carry on baggage, headed to the car rental agency. They rented an American sedan and made their way down Nimitz Highway, past Ala Moana Beach Park and the Ala Wai Boat Harbor and into the heart of Waikiki. They checked into a room overlooking the beach. After they unpacked and had a simple dinner in the hotel coffee shop, they turned in for the night.

Tomorrow would be a big day.

The next morning, the couple got up early and slipped out the side door of their hotel and had breakfast at a different hotel restaurant. After breakfast, they walked east towards Diamond Head and entered an ABC Store. They paid cash for gaudy tourist attire, complete with loud Hawaiian shirts and shorts, hats, and matching bright red oversized sunglasses. They kept walking and when they reached the Hyatt Regency, slipped into the lobby restrooms and changed into their new clothes.

Back in the lobby, the man spied their reflection in the gift shop window. "We look like idiots."

She glanced at him. "And unrecognizable."

Across the street, they waited in front of the King Kalākaua statue to catch the Waikiki Trolley to Chinatown.

The couple had done their homework before leaving for the islands, going online and studying the streets and their names. They had even walked the neighborhood virtually using Google Earth. They knew where to park, where to eat, and where to avoid.

As they rode, the woman read from a pamphlet she found in the lobby of their hotel. "Listen to this. There was an outbreak of bubonic plague in Chinatown in October 1899. In January 1900, the Board of Health set forty-one fires to stop the outbreak. The wind came up, the fires spread and burned out of control for seventeen days and burned thirty-eight acres."

"I think burning down Chinatown is overkill. Even for us," the man whispered to her.

The trolly meandered its way through Honolulu, finally turning on Smith Street and then turned again on King Street.

When the trolly stopped at the corner of Bethel Street and King Street, the couple got off and found themselves across the street from Walmart.

They walked for a while, looking for an address.

"This is the place," the man said, stopping in front of a restaurant and gesturing to the building across the street with dirty windows and peeling paint.

"What a pit," the woman said.

Stairs beside the store led to the second floor apartments above a Chinese grocery store.

They walked up and down the street, looking in shop windows while keeping an eye on the front of the building. The man checked his watch; it was a few minutes after eleven. He turned and saw a Thai restaurant behind him. "This is a good place to keep an eye out. We can see the entrance from here. How about we have an early lunch?"

They were seated at a table in the front window. They read the menus and ordered. When the waitress was out of earshot, the woman said, "You have to be the only vegetarian in this business."

"There are a few of us. We have a group that meets once a year."

The woman pulled a copy of the Honolulu Star Advertiser from her purse. She flipped through the newspaper, skimming through the news articles. She stopped, turned the paper towards the man, and pointed. He leaned forward and read.

A 35-year-old Caucasian male who was stabbed in Chinatown has died from his injuries at Queen's Hospital. Honolulu Police say the incident, apparently drug-related, occurred around 9:30 p.m. on Friday near Hotel Street and Nu'uanu Avenue. Police do not have a suspect at this time and are asking anyone who has information to call the Crime Stoppers hotline.

"We make it look like a drug deal gone bad?" he asked.

"Works for me. We get our business done, ditch these awful clothes, and get on with our vacation."

"One thing you can say for Raphael, he pays well when the job is done—or kills you if you mess up."

She laughed. "That's two things."

The food came and they ate.

"There he is." She gestured towards the building across the street with her chopsticks. Darby Jurgis emerged from the doorway at the base of the stairs.

"Look at those clothes. That suit is barely hanging off of him. He looks homeless. The guy is a mess," the man said.

"I think we are supposed to say 'houseless' now and not 'homeless'. I don't think a bad drug deal would be too hard to sell," she said, taking a bite of bamboo shoot.

"Houseless? I can't keep up," said the man.

Chapter Fifty-Four

Nick closed up *Icarus* and caught the plane to Maui. The rest of the crew would arrive later that day or the next.

Saturday, Nick and Willie inspected *Caprice* and readied her for the race on Monday. They provisioned with food and supplies, and by nine o'clock they walked to town.

"Wow, look at the traffic," Willie said, "I remember when this was a sleepy little tourist town."

They spent Saturday walking around Lahaina and sitting in cafés.

"You know, the first Chinese in Hawaii settled in Lahaina. They came here to work in the sandalwood trade. That was in the late 1700s. Most of them were men and they married Hawaiian women. That's why so many Chinese in Hawaii have Hawaiian blood," Willie said.

"I always learn something interesting when I am with you," Nick said.

On Sunday, Willie and Nick headed to a nearby park with a backgammon set, while Nigel, Helena, Charlotte, Tina, and Chad took in a movie to get out of the heat.

"I got a call from Gretchen," Willie said, rolling the dice.

"Uh, oh."

"Yeah. She was steamed. Said you broke it off and kicked her off the boat." Willie moved a couple of pieces.

"That's not the way it happened." Nick took his turn and rolled double sixes.

"I figured there was more to it than that."

"Why did she call you? I didn't realize you two were close."

"We aren't. She needed to vent and I am the only one she knows that knows you." Willie took his turn.

"She told me we didn't have a future with her needing to finish her medical degree and all that went with it. I couldn't think of any reason to postpone the agony of parting."

Nick rolled the dice.

"Double sixes again? You sure are lucky."

Nick moved more pieces.

Willie picked up the dice and rolled a three and a four. "She said you said, and I think I have this right, 'I think we should stop spending time together by Friday'."

Nick winced.

"So she left."

"Yes, that's about right," Nick admitted.

"Seems harsh."

"I needed to get her off the boat."

Willie looked sideways at his friend. "There's more to the story than you're telling me. This isn't the Nick Thomas I know. You've had a cloud hanging over you for the last month. First you want to talk to someone discreetly about a gemstone, and now this."

"I can't talk about it."

"Does this have anything to do with my cousin Leland Chan?"

"I can't talk about it," Nick said, head down, studying the board.

By Sunday night, the bar at the Lahaina Yacht Club was in high gear. It's the wildest night of the season, the last night of Race Week and the night before the Lahaina Return. Sounds of the rowdy sailing crowd on the deck of the club floated across the water to *Caprice* on their offshore mooring.

The boats were divided into six classes with staggered start times, depending on the type of boat and handicap. The non-spinnaker and slowest boats started first, the multihulls, the fastest, started last. Boats heading to Kaneohe, the alternate finish line on the windward side of Oahu, like *Caprice*, started second to last.

The race began much earlier than Willie's normal wake up time and he announced to the crew he would adjourn at midnight and climb out of his bunk for coffee and get to the starting line.

That was if he could sleep from the noise. Some crews stayed up and drank all night and continued that way for the entire race the following morning. The trick was to have fun, but not too much fun, and still be fresh enough to compete in the next day's race. It was usually an easy sail after a challenging week of more complicated racing. Boats had most of their sails flying for the push downwind to Oahu and stereos played on the decks, only drowned out by blenders making boat drinks.

Then there were the serious racers. They tuned their boats

and inspected hardware before the race. They often had matching shirts, shorts, and hats. Willie's crew fell somewhere between the extremes of the racers and the up-all-night crews.

The next morning *Caprice*, with Willie at the helm and Nick acting as tactician, was the first in their class across the starting line. The trade winds had shifted and Catamarans are not known for sailing well into the wind. Nick suggested they set their course to go along Moloka'i's north shore. They would pass the highest sea cliffs in the world, instead of the usual route to Honolulu, along Moloka'i's south shore.

They stayed in the Pailolo Channel between Maui and Moloka'i and rounded the west end of Moloka'i. *Pailolo* translates to "crazy fisherman", and the channel is considered the windiest and roughest in the Hawaiian Islands. That morning the trip, while exciting and requiring vigilance, was not dangerous. Soon they were abeam Hālawa Valley, one of the oldest settlements in Hawaii, dating back more than 1,300 years. On the other side of Moloka'i, the boats had entered *the slot*, the part of the Kalohi Channel between the island of Lanai and Moloka'i. The boats in the slot experienced constant 25 knot winds with gusts to 35, not uncommon for the islands. Nick saw two other catamarans also taking the northern route.

Nick stood at the helm for most of the trip. They spread the rest of the crew around the boat, on the bow, in the cockpit, and in the main cabin. Young Chad sat with Nick in the elevated helm station. Willie was in the stateroom, reading *West With the Night*, the memoir of the English-born Kenyan aviatrix, Beryl Markham.

As they passed Hālawa Valley, Willie came into the cockpit

and stood behind Nick at the wheel. "Did you know Beryl Markham became the first person to fly solo, non-stop across the Atlantic from Britain to North America in 1936?" he asked.

"How about that?" Nick said, glancing over at two other catamarans running nearly even with *Caprice*.

Willie looked at the other boats and up at the spinnaker. He pondered for a moment and dropped below. A moment later, he emerged from the forward hatch with a large sail bag. He had an odd expression on his face.

"Secret weapon," he said when Nick gave him a "what gives?" look.

"Nigel," Willie called. "You're a crazy foredeck guy. How about giving me a hand?"

Nigel joined Willie, and they dropped the spinnaker through the hatch.

Nick noticed the boat slow down. "If you guys don't hurry doing what you're doing, the other boats will pass us."

Willie and Nigel raised the other sail.

"What kind of sail is that?" Chad asked, looking at the strange shape.

"It's a gennaker," Nick said.

"A what?"

A gennaker. It's like a spinnaker, but asymmetrical like a genoa. A genoa is a large foresail or jib that overlaps the main-sail. A gennaker is something between a spinnaker and a genoa, and is good for a beam reach, like we're on now, when the wind comes across the side of the boat.

With the sail set, Willie made his way back to the cockpit. "If we are going to race, we might as well race to win," he said, looking up at the sails. He moved forward to make adjustments.

"I've never seen him like this," Nigel said to Nick, joining them at the helm.

Nick felt the increase in speed and turned into his tactician persona. "Willie, take the helm and come up two degrees. Nigel, give me a quarter turn on the gennaker. Helena move outboard on the port side, everybody else stay where they are." Nick moved forward, eased the mainsail, and adjusted the boom vang and downhaul. The minor changes added up to more speed. Nick checked out the other boats. *Caprice* was already pulling away from them. He tapped Willie on the shoulder and pointed to the knotmeter.

"Wow," Willie said, "We are going really fast."

Their boat speed was 19 knots and increasing.

"Don't screw up at this speed, okay? We could do real damage," Willie warned.

"I'm on it," Nick replied, scanning the boat and sails. Nick knew in that wind and at that speed there was no room for error. If the wind shifted, it could send the main sail violently across the boat in an uncontrolled jibe.

"Stay sharp everybody. Call out if anything doesn't look right. I mean anything," Nick announced to the crew.

Nick moved about the boat, constantly tuning while keeping Willie informed so he could change the heading for optimal speed. *Caprice* plowed through the sea, passing the bays and inlets on the north shore. They approached the cliffs of Moloka'i and the Kalaupapa Peninsula, home of the leper colony once attended to by Belgian Priest Father Damien.

Nick and Willie and Nigel worked as a team to keep the speed of the boat at its fastest. The crew watched the other boats get smaller as *Caprice* pulled ahead. By the time they passed the northwest tip of Moloka'i, they left the other boats far behind.

"Take a look, Willie," Nick said, handing the binoculars to him.

The boats on the other side of Moloka'i in the Kaiwi Channel sailed on a rhumb line for Diamond Head and their finish line. *Caprice* kept their course for their finish at Kaneohe.

Willie handed the binoculars back to Nick. "Take the wheel. This is too much work." Willie took one last look to the stern and went below, crawled into his bunk and was asleep in a few moments.

Nick took the opportunity to teach the finer points of sailing to any crew who wanted to learn. Chad was the first in line. Nick sat him at the helm and let him drive the boat, keeping a light hand on the wheel. Some people have a knack for finding the groove on a sailboat, and like Gretchen, Chad was a natural. Once he sat down and took the wheel, he stayed on course, and Nick showed him how to gauge the wind and the waves.

Nick took the binoculars hanging from the binnacle and scanned the horizon. He saw other boats sailing for Kaneohe had taken *the slot*. The plan to take the north route paid off, and they were ahead of the pack.

That afternoon, with Chad still at the wheel, they raced toward the finish line.

"Somebody wake up Willie and tell him the race is over," Nick said as the race committee boat, with a blast of an air horn, signaled *Caprice* crossing between their boat and the finish mark.

Willie came up on the deck, groggy from sleeping through the race.

"We won, Willie. We beat the other multihulls," Nick told him.

"How about that?" He let out a yawn.

"I still think yacht racing is a stupid sport."

Chapter Fifty-Five

Tuesday morning, back on *Icarus*, Nick had just taken the housing off of the compass when his mobile phone rang.

"You're back on your boat," Chan said.

"Yes. I got in last night," Nick replied.

"Have you been in touch with anybody at the company since you got back?"

"No. I haven't talked to any of them since I climbed out the window."

"Yeah, we saw that. Nice exit."

"It's nice that you're looking out for me," Nick said.

"Darby Jurgis has gone missing. Was he planning a business trip or something?"

"Not that I'm aware of, but he isn't involved with the day-to-day operations of the company. I don't know what he does when he's not scheming with Blaine," Nick said.

"Stick around the boat. We're on our way there. We need to go over a few details before we proceed with arrests."

"Okay. I'll be here."

Nick was fiddling with a connection to the compass light in the binnacle when the gate to the dock slammed shut. When he looked up a few moments later, Blaine was standing on the dock below him. He was wearing a light blue jacket, which Nick considered odd on a warm morning. Sweat dripped down Blaine's face.

Nick stepped from under the dodger and toward the companionway. As Blaine came closer, Nick caught a menacing glint in the man's moist eyes.

"Blaine. What are you doing here?"

"Look, Nick, I know you were the one that called the FBI. I didn't believe it at first, because of what you did in San Francisco. You and your partner, Lance, was it? I figured you got away with the money and stashed it somewhere, headed to the islands like a lot of others on this rock."

"That's not how it happened. You've got it wrong," Nick said.

"I was going through the medical billing program and noticed changes to the code I made. Someone had redirected the money to other offshore companies. The amounts were bigger and more frequent. I figured Big Jack was the only one who could have figured it out and he wanted a piece of the action."

Nick heard the gate slam once more, but kept his focus on Blaine.

"So I tell Big Jack I know what he's doing, and he says you know all about it and you took him to meet with the FBI. Big Jack figured if he moved a lot of money quickly, he would have money hidden away before the FBI shut it down. I'd get blamed, and he'd be in the clear."

Nick stood listening to Blaine's confession. He tightened the grip on the screwdriver in his hand.

"I tell Big Jack there's more money than that flowing through the company, and if he teams up with me, we can make a bundle and each go our own way. This morning I took him out on my friend's boat to have a private talk without interruptions."

Nick shook his head. *Big Jack came to me for help and then sold me out. Will I ever learn?*

"How did that go?" Nick asked.

"Fine, although it turns out Big Jack couldn't swim," Blaine said, pulling a pistol from his jacket pocket and pointing it at Nick.

"Aloha, Nick," he said, pulling the trigger.

Nick saw the flash, heard the bang, and felt the pain at the same moment.

Blaine's hands holding the gun trembled and his eyes wobbled. He let out an agonizing groan and collapsed.

Nick saw John Mitchell standing at the end of the dock, still in a shooting stance. Behind him, Leland Chan rushed forward, pushing Mitchell's aiming arms away as he passed him. He got to Blaine and kicked the gun out of his reach. Mitchell re-holstered his gun and rushed to check on Nick, who was hunched over, holding his side, blood on his hands and shirt.

"I thought Chan had someone watching me," Nick said, his face contorted.

Mitchell climbed on board. "He did, and they were supposed to take up their positions last night when you returned. I think heads are going to roll."

"I'm glad it wasn't *my* head that rolled," Nick said. "Thank's for that."

"Let me look," Mitchell said.

Wincing, Nick lifted the bottom of his shirt.

Mitchell examined the wound. "It's through-and-through. A few inches to the left and you would be in real trouble."

Mitchell looked down at Chan, who was examining Blaine. Chan looked up at Mitchell, shook his head, and dialed his mobile phone.

Nick reached into the lazarette for a first aid kit and a bottle of rum. He took a swig from the bottle and handed the kit to Mitchell.

"Do you mind doing the honors?"

"Okay. Then we should get you to the hospital to make sure the bullet didn't hit anything vital."

Nick heard sirens in the distance. He turned and saw the slug lodged in the molding on the companionway. "Damn it, I just refinished that wood."

"I'm glad you have your priorities straight," Mitchell said as he began bandaging the holes in Nick Thomas.

Nick Thomas will return in
NINE DAYS IN MILAN

About the Author

Patrick Livanos Lester is a writer, artist, and gemologist. He was a senior flight and ground operations engineer on NASA's space station and shuttle programs and an international business consultant. He knows his way around boats and airplanes and lives with his wife Kim in California and Hawaii and other places with sailboats and palm trees.

Check out the Rhumbline Press website at www.rhumblinepress.com. It has book and music reviews, photos and tidbits, relevant and not, to his books. Sign up for Patrick's newsletter and receive the free e-book *Caviar Stories: A Short History to Caviar*.

You can find original content on Patrick's Instagram feed at www.instagram.com/patricklivanoslester and at Facebook at www.facebook.com/patrick.livanoslester

Reviews are very important to authors. If you enjoyed *Strange Weather in Chinatown*, please consider leaving a review on Amazon—it would be greatly appreciated.

You can also send Patrick an email via www.rhumblinepress.com, which he will answer personally.

Made in the USA
Monee, IL
21 April 2022

94861521R00142